17 More Days
By
Michael J May

Part II of the 17 Days Series

Contents

Intro.
Day 1, Monday, 17th of March.
Day 2, Tuesday, 18th of March.
Day 3, Wednesday, 19th of March.
Day 4, Thursday, 20th of March.
Day 5, Friday, 21st of March.
Day 6, Saturday, 22nd of March.
Day 7, Sunday, 23rd of March.
Day 8, Monday, 24th of March.
Day 9, Tuesday, 25th of March.
Day 10, Wednesday, 26th of March.
Day 11, Thursday, 27th of March.
Day 12, Thursday, 28th of March.
Day 13, Friday, 29th of March.
Day 14, Saturday, 30th of March.
Day 15, Sunday, 31st of March.
Day 16, Monday, 1st of April.
Day 17, Tuesday, 2nd of April.
Outro

INTRO.

Hi. Remember me? Jack? You hopefully just finished reading 17 Days, which was an account of the final 17 days before my Decree Absolute.

Welcome to *17 More Days*, where we follow on from these events, picking up where we left off.

Rather than dealing with the depressive issues of the divorce process, this story will deal with the immediate aftermath, and the difficulties of starting a new life/family. We will still talk about anxiety, worries, issues, problems, etc. as the mental health issues play a crucial part in this series of books.

Cut, paste, and update of the Intro to *17 Days*:

Meet Jack; 41 years young, has 2 wonderful kids, a lovely wife, and basically a great life. Sounds great. Took some time to get here though following his divorce. This book basically is a day-by-day account of the 17 days following receipt of the Decree Absolute, signalling his freedom.

Why bother? Well, I think it's important to show you the immediate aftermath of a divorce; life was complicated. A constant juggling act.

MRMICHAELJOSEPHMAY

Hope you enjoy and are able to identify.

DAY 1

Monday, 17th of March.

Heart about to explode....Deep breath. Go....
"Guys, I'd like you to meet Chrissy"
That's where we left things at the end of 17 Days. I was introducing my kids to Chrissy, which was one of the most nerve-racking moments of my life. This will be a short-ish chapter, as it was 1700 when we left the story.

Here's what happened next.

"Hi, nice to see you again" said James
"Hi" Elsie said, a bit uncertain.
"Hello, I'm Chrissy, nice to see you again James. And very nice to finally meet you Elsie." She extended her hand "You're even prettier than your dad told me" she winked "And I *love* your hair"
Elsie smiled and shook her hand "Thank you, I did it myself"
"Wow, maybe you can help me with mine sometime, I'm useless" she ruffled her own hair.
"That would be nice" Elsie said, more confidently.
"Great. Would you guys like anything to eat and

drink?"
Smiles all round.
"Yes please, I'm starving" James
"Yes please" Elsie added.
"Go pick whatever you want, my treat" Chrissy said.
The kids ran back over and started talking excitedly among themselves, pointing at things on the menu board.

"You're a natural" I said to Chrissy, I put my hand on her shoulder and smiled.
"Wow. I was terrified. You think they like me?" she was genuinely worried. "James seems ok, but not sure about Elsie" she added.
"Hey. You did well. It takes Elsie a bit of time to warm to anyone. You made her smile, that's a start."
"I really hope so Jack. I'd hate for your kids to dislike me, or see me as an evil interloper"
"I'm sure they'll be fine" I replied reassuringly Just give them time"
"I'm petrified. I just want to make a good impression"
"Well, bribing with food and drink is a good start" I joked
"Not funny. You think that's what they're thinking? Dammit" She started nervously picking at her nails.
"Hey, relax. Pretty sure that's not what they're thinking"
"You sure? I'd hate for the…" I cut her off and took her hand in mine.

"Stop. It's all good. Just relax and be you"
"Sorry. I'm so nervous"
"Understood. They can be little buggers sometime" I winked
"Wha...?" But the kids cut her off before she could finish
"We've ordered hot chocolates with cream, and sprinkles, and marshmallow!" Elsie said excitedly
"Ooh good choice" Chrissy said with a big smile.
First tangent time!

You think this was all moving really fast, and it was far too soon to introduce the kids?
Possibly.
But.

Reasoning:

1. I felt that my relationship with Chrissy was only going to grow stronger (it would; we got married obviously), and I didn't think it was either workable, or fair to try keep it a secret.

2. I was also confident that my kids were mature enough to see that their father couldn't be on his own forever. He'd already been alone for almost 9 months. Whereas their mother had been in a relationship since day 1 of her intent to leave.

3. I had faith in my brood. They are kind-hearted, loving children. I had discussed it with Chrissy that morning, and she was slightly reluctant, but had gone along with it. I had given her some pointers, clothes, hair (she was obsessed with doing her hair in different ways at the moment), usual girl stuff.

4. Let's be honest; she'd already met James, so it seemed a bit weird not to include Elsie.

What do you think? Good enough? Well, it was for me. How long did you wait until you introduced your partner to your kids? You think it was too early, just right, or that you waited too long? Different for everyone. Hindsight is also a wonderful thing eh…

Meanwhile, in the story…..

I stood, and pulled chairs out "Here guys, have a seat"
Imagine my surprise when Elsie sat in my chair, right next to Chrissy.
Chrissy and I exchanged a shocked look "Oh, ok, take my seat why don't you" I said to Elsie jokingly.
"You sit over there on the boy's side of the table" she replied, pointing at the other 2 chairs.
"Oh, I see, like that now is it?" I laughed "Ok, ok" I sat next to James.

And so we sat, for the best part of an hour; James and I talking about football and school, Elsie and Chrissy having in depth discussions about hair styling (with photo backup from Elsie's phone)
"Hey guys" I said eventually, "Think it's time to let Chrissy go now, and we should go home for dinner."
"Daddy?" Elsie asked coyly
"Yes?"
"Can Chrissy have dinner with us?"
"I don't know" turning to Chrissy "Can you?"
Somewhat taken aback, Chrissy said "Sure. I'd love

to"
"Yeay!" both kids seemed more than happy.
"Great. Go say bye to Uncle Steve before we go"
The kids ran off to tackle Steve, who was more than happy to receive hugs from them.
I turned to Chrissy "Wow. Get you, Miss popular"
"Oh my God. I'm soooooo relieved. She's soooooo adorable"
"Takes after her dad?" I offered...
"That's pushing it a bit" she replied laughing.
And so we went home and had dinner. As our new family group. And it was great. It was fantastic.
I was so happy that both kids had taken to Chrissy.

Imagine if it went the other way! Wow. If it did for you, you have my sympathy. It's the hardest thing in the world to do, and if it then doesn't go well.... doesn't bare thinking about. I was lucky. If you weren't, I hope it's all good now. If it's too early to tell; I hope it gets better.

The kids were disappointed when it was time for Chrissy to go home; James gave her a hug, and Elsie made her promise she could do her hair next time.
"Absolutely" Chrissy reassured her "I'd love that"
After she had left, we did our chores, and I called a family meeting.

"So, you two. Talk to me" I said
"She's tidy dad, well done" James offered.
"Wow. Ok, thanks mate" I said "Good to know" No worries there...
I looked at Elsie "And you?"
"Well, I don't know..." she said

Surprised, and slightly worried, I asked "Why, what's wrong?"

"I'm kidding dad" she laughed. "I like her, she has *really* nice hair"

Big sigh of relief "You scare me sometimes Ello" I said with a smile

She laughed mischievously. "Sorry"

"She was really nervous and worried about meeting you" I said. "We both were"

I continued "But I'm happy it went well. And I'm so very proud of you both. Thank you"

We had a group hug and watched a bit of tv before bedtime.

"Right, you two, bed. School tomorrow" I said.

"Dad! It's only 8 o'clock" Protests.

"Hey, you have to catch the bus to Ramsey don't forget, so you'll have to get up a bit earlier"

Reluctantly, they both gave goodnight hugs and disappeared upstairs for teeth and bed.

"Night guys, love you"

I went to the fridge and got myself a beer. And took a moment. If you have anxiety, you'll possibly identify with the following narrative.

I needed some time to relax. I was exhausted. Not physically, but mentally. My mind had been going at a million miles an hour all day. All these thoughts, doubts, worries, concerns whirling around like a hurricane, jostling for attention. Inner voice just giving you loads of abuse, bombarding you with self-doubt and self-loathing. It's EXHAUSTING. Both physically and mentally. I was tired. My head was done for the day. I sat and did a few breathing exercises, trying to calm my mind before bed. I really didn't want to be awake all night; time to muzzle the inner voice. My beer sat un-touched, and I had a message from Chrissy. I was too exhausted for either.

I went up to bed, put my headphones in; Mycroft was expecting me at the Diogenes Club.

Zzzzzzzzz.......

DAY 2

Tuesday, 18th of March.

I was awake before the alarm went off, still dark outside. I lay and thought about the events of the previous day, which did miracles for my mood. I got out of bed full of happiness, got dressed, and went down to make the kids pancakes. Nice hearty breakfast to set them up for the day. Kids eventually drifted into the kitchen, and we sat down to eat. Elsie was not a morning person, like her mother. She was quiet, and looked like she could just get back into bed and sleep the rest of the day. James, on the other hand, was spritely and chatty. Deffo a morning person like his dad I thought. (Minus the chatty part perhaps…)

After breakfast, the kids showered, dressed, and rushed out of the door. "Bye guys!" "Bye dad! Love you!" And they were gone; off into their own stories. No run this morning, too full of pancakes; I'd do one later this evening. I cleared the dishes and made myself a coffee. I sat at the table for a while, just thinking up a work schedule for today. I had a lot to do, so needed to get stuck in. And to stay positive. *We'll see about that.* No, I will.

What is there to be negative about? Everything is going well. *Is it? What about your ex-wife Jacko?* Why would I worry about that? *She saw you with another woman.* We're divorced! *Yes, but how do you think it made her feel?* I know how she felt; I could see it in her eyes. *You fucking destroyed her life Jack.* No! She did that herself! She destroyed MY life. *You saw that look on her face Jacky boy, she'll be out for revenge.* What? How? *She controls access to the kid's lad, don't forget that.* Shut up dammit, she can't do that! We have an agreement. *She'll find a way.....* Fuck off. Leave me alone.

Angry with myself, and the voice in my fucking head, I picked up my phone. Shit. I didn't respond to Chrissy last night. *Ha! You've done it now fuckwit, she'll drop you like a rock!* "Would you just fuck off already!" I shouted. Out loud. At no-one. I looked around at the empty room. Jesus, Jack, get a grip. I called Chrissy, but it went straight to answerphone. Probably work I thought. *Or is she just ignoring you?* No. Not having it. I went upstairs and lost myself in work. Not time for inner voice whilst working, my mind would be fully engaged.

Like an absolute boss, I'd finished 3 videos by one o'clock. Good effort. I was pleased. I called Chrissy, still no answer. *Ha! Fuck yeah! See?* Would you fuck off! Dammit. No. No. No. Not happening today. I went up and grabbed my laptops. Sitting in the café would be better for me at the moment. It was still cold out, but not as cold as last week. Soon, the snow would be gone, and we'd be back to normal. Whatever normal is.

Made my way to the Willow Tree Cafe (rhymes!), where I was greeted by Willow.

"Hi Jack. Didn't expect to see you here for a few days" She said cheerfully

"Wasn't having a great time at home" I said "Needed to be around people"

"Ah, cool. Well, have a seat and I'll get you a drink and some lunch."

"Thanks Willow. Steve out?" I took off my coat, and set up my office at my usual table.

"Yeah, he's had to drive out to the city to see his Mum. She's had a bit of a turn"

"Oh no, nothing bad I hope?"

"I don't really know to be honest, he hasn't really talked about her much" she said, with a hint of concern.

"She went into sheltered accommodation a few years ago after his dad passed away. Her eyesight isn't too good anymore." I explained

"Ah. Poor dear, I hope she's ok" she said concerned.

"We're about to find out" I said, spotting Steve's car pulling around the corner.

"Ooh, he's back" She smiled, her mood instantly better. *These two are made for each other* I thought.

A few moments later, the man himself entered.

"Hey buddy!" he said, surprised to see me. He walked over to Willow, and gave her a kiss. "Hi you."

"Hi yourself" she said and hugged him.

"Wasn't expecting to see you for a bit" he said hanging his coat up. "Wait a minute. You ok?"

"Not really mate, but coming here helps I guess" Admission. Don't be afraid to open up to people who care. Ever.

He walked over and gave me a big hug "Always good to see you buddy" he said

"And you man" I answered.

He walked over to get a bottle of water from the fridge. "How's your ma?" I asked

"She's ok mate. Had a fall bless her. Sprained her ankle and took a bit of a knock to the head."

"Ouch. She in hospital?"

"Nah, she's resting at home. The carers come and check on her every hour, she's in good hands"

"That's good to hear" I said with relief. "Hope you don't mind, but I told Willow about your ma, she was worried"

"Yeah, "he said with a sigh. "It's been tough finding time to sit and just chat about stuff you know? Always busy here." he said waving his hand around.

"Why don't you take a few days off and take her somewhere nice?" I asked

"Close the caff?" he said incredulously.

"Dude. You can well afford to close for a few days. People will live"

"Really? I thought they depended on me" he said jokingly. "Fair enough mate, I'll have a think"

"Good lad. It'll be good for you to have some time off to relax" I said "It's important"

"Yeah, you're right. I find somewhere nice to go"

"Effort. Now fuck off and leave me alone, I have a shit tonne of work to get through" I said

"Fucking hell. Alright mate, calm down, I'm leaving" He laughed, and went back to talk to Willow.

I turned back to my laptop. Right. Coffee? Check. Sandwich? Check? Ok, let's do this. I put headphones on and disappeared into the world of content editing.

A few hours later, or more, I wasn't sure; I'd lost track of time, there was a tap on my shoulder. I took the headphones off.

"Mate, it's almost 5." Steve said, tapping his watch "Stop milking my Wi-Fi and go the fuck home already"

"Shit, yeah, sorry mate. Gimme a sec" I shut down, and packed my stuff.

"You really get lost in that stuff don't you?" he asked

"Yeah, I tune out of reality and concentrate 100% on it. That way, there's no space for demons in my thoughts"

"You're a fucking fruit loop" he ruffled my hair. "Now get out. We want to go home"

I turned to see Willow standing by the counter, coat on, waiting to go. She smiled and waved.

"Fuck. Sorry guys" I apologised.

"No worries Jack" Willow said. "He's giving me a lift home, otherwise you would have been ok"

I put my coat on, apologised again, and left them to close up and go home.

It was too early to go home and vegetate, and the demons would come back if I did, so I went for a walk to kill some time. In my head, I was going over what I needed to do this week work-wise, and in the end worked out that I had enough time to finish all the projects. Pfew. That was a bit of a relief. I realised I had forgotten to ask Steve how he got on with Ken and his finance/legal stuff; I made a mental note to speak to him about it tomorrow. Looking around me, it was one of those typical grey, overcast days, still pretty cold, and the snow was still there. Everything looks so much better with snow, it's truly beautiful. It also lifted my mood. I walked along the canal, which was mostly deserted. There were a few other walkers out, and I spotted a few guys fishing on the other side. The delicate crunch of the snow underfoot was the only sound in my ears. Peaceful. Bliss. Just what my mind needed. I made a few snowballs and threw them aimlessly at trees. I was loving it. But it also made me think of my kids. Shit. *Let's not go there Jack.* I thought, and was about to chastise myself when.....bang! Snowball to the back of the head. "The fuck??" I shouted out and turned to see which little shitbag had thrown it at me.

"Hey you" big smile. Anger instantly dissipated; it was Chrissy.

"Wow, good shot" I said, rubbing the back of my head.

"Sorry, I was aiming for your back" she said laughing

"Your aim needs some work"

She closed the distance and gave me a hug. It felt good to be in her arms. It felt good to be in anybody's arms. But she smelled better than "anybody".

"You ok?" she asked, with a hint of concern. *Probably because you hugged so hard and she thinks you're desperate!* Shut up inner voice! *Lol, funny. Inner voice telling inner voice to fuck off? You're losing it.*

"Yeah, been a bit up and down all day, but far better now" I replied

"I do have that effect on people" she said, smarmily.

"Works in this case" I said and hugged her again. "It's good to see you"

"And you" she smiled "Looks like I got here just in time"

"Yeah you did. Want to walk?"

"Please. I need a break from work" she said

"Busy day?"

"Yeah, it's going to be one of those weeks" she said

"Know how that feels" I replied.

"It's so beautiful here" she said "I'm glad I moved down"

"Me too. It's nice to have you close" *Whoa! Steady on there cowboy.* Fuck off!

"Nice to hear I didn't move down for nothing" she smiled and kissed me.

I looked around to see if anyone was about, not sure why I did that, but she noticed.

She put her hands on my face and said "Hey, you don't need to worry about that. You're single now, remember?"

"Yeah. I'm sorry" I apologised.

"Well, you're technically *not* single I suppose, you're mine now" she winked

Tangent.

Wait. I'm hers now? Hers? I went from being married to being with someone else quite quickly. Was it quick though? I had been alone for almost 9 months. It that enough time? Is that what people were thinking? Is that what the kids would be thinking? Ffs. I didn't know. I thought the kids were ok with it, in fact, I'm sure they were, so no worries there. What about everyone else? Do they think I've jumped straight into another relationship? These were the thoughts in my mind, and likely in your mind too if you found yourself in a similar situation. Would my new relationship be accepted by friends & family? Fuck. What about my parents? What would they think? Would they like Chrissy? Did they still like Helen? Did they miss her? I'd never really spoken to them about it. Maybe I should. Life is never simple. If you're a divorced dad, it never will be again. Trust me.

Back in the room...

"Earth to Jack?"
"Wha...?"
"Wow, where were you?" She asked
"Sorry, just lost in thought" I added meekly. *You need to do better than that Jack!* Yeah, ok...
"Hey, you have time for a drink?" I asked
"Erm, yeah, sure" she looked at her watch.
"You sure? I mean, we can do it another time" I was rambling....
"It's ok" she said "Just checking the time was all. Aunt Mary gets back from her friends around 7, so I have time"
"Thanks" I said with more than a hint of relief. "I'd like to talk to you about some stuff"
"Oh dear, should I be worried?" she asked

"No, just stuff I need to share is all" I replied with a smile.

We walked back to the village, and to the George.

I got us both a pint of local ale, and we found a table away from the bar.

"So, "Chrissy said as she took off her coat "What was it you wanted to talk about?"

"I want to start off by saying that I'm coming into this relationship with the utmost sincerity, not just a rebound"

"I appreciate that" she winked

"I'm trying to be serious!" I said

"Sorry, carry on"

"Anyway, I wanted you to know that I want this relationship to be based purely on truth and trust"

"Agreed" she nodded

"I want to be able to tell you anything, regardless of how difficult it might be"

She took my hand and said "Jack, I want exactly the same. I'm tired of being lied to, and tiptoed around. You're saying all the right things"

"Thank you" I said meekly. "It's important to me to be able to tell you anything I need to. There's a lot going on in my head."

"I have a feeling you'd like to get started right away?" she said. More of a question than a statement.

"Yes, I have some stuff I want to get out if that's ok?" I asked tentatively

"You can tell me anything, as long as you're not breaking up with me"

"You're kidding, I can tell" I winked.

"Anyway, a few things are worrying me. I'm happy

to be with you, and I'm with you for all the right reasons." I started.
"Good"
"But. I have niggles in my head. Would you mind if I just asked you some questions? It's probably easier than me rambling on incoherently"
"Whatever is easiest for you" she said, and leaned forward, the attentive listener.
"Ok, question one. Do you think we're getting together too soon?"
"Too soon after the divorce?" she countered
I nodded "Yes"
"If you had been together until the day of the absolute, then yes. But you were alone for almost 9 months Jack. That's plenty of time for me to know it's not some rebound reaction"
"Thank you. Ok, question 2. Do you think the kids mind me being with another woman?"
"Your kids seem genuinely happy that you are not alone anymore Jack. And I think they like me, so no, I don't think they mind at all"
I sighed deeply "That's good to hear"
"I'm no expert on kids Jack, but they seem really happy for you."
"Good. I think so too, I just can't see it from the outside. Ok, next question. Do you think other people will think it's too soon?"
She thought for a moment, then replied "To be honest with you Jack, I don't really care what other people think. I'm not sure who you mean by "other people" but Steve and Willow are happy, my Aunt Mary is happy. Who else is there that you should be worried about?" She paused, then "Ah. Your

parents"
"Yes. I'm completely unsure what to think. I haven't talked to them about the divorce, so I don't know what their feelings are about it. Do they blame me? Do they miss Helen? Will they dislike the fact that I'm in another relationship? I have no idea."
"You know what Jack?" she asked
"What?"
"There's only one way to find out. Come on" She stood and put her coat on.
"Where you going?" I asked
"*You*, are taking *me* to see your parents. Now" She ordered. *Oh shit...*
"Now?" I asked uneasy. *Fucking hell Jack...*
"Yes, now. They only live up the road. Come on." She took my hand and led me outside.
"But, they don't know I'm coming" I said weakly, my anxiety alarm ringing LOUDLY.
"Time to man up Jack. They're retired, they'll be home." she said, dragging me along
We walked the short distance over the bridge to my folk's house.
Outside, I stood with my finger hovering over the bell, still unsure, and partially unwilling.
"Allow me" she said and knocked on the door.

Let me take a moment to tell you how I was feeling: I was *shitting* myself. Holy crap. I wasn't ready. I needed time to prepare! *Shut up you dick, just get on with it!* And YOU can fuck off and all! Bloody inner voice. My anxiety was all over the place; my stomach was a mess, and my hands were shaking.

Ok, moment over, dad is opening the door.

"Oh hi son (looks from me to Chrissy, and back to me, puzzled), wasn't expecting you, come in. "
He stood aside, and let us in. "Barbara, Jack's here" he called out to mum.
I walked into the living room, where my mum was already getting out of her chair. "Oh hi Jack, lovely surprise" she beamed. Pause. "And who's this?" Dad had joined us, and stood next to mum. Their faces were blank; this was going to fucking bomb.
"Mum, dad, this is Chrissy" I said hesitantly
"Hi, very nice to meet you" Chrissy said, shaking hands.
"Hi Chrissy, nice to meet you" mum said, looking from Chrissy to me. *Shit.*
"Chrissy is..." I paused, lost for the right words.
"I'm Jack's new girlfriend" Chrissy finished for me.
"Ooh, how lovely" mum said, looking slightly unsure. *Fuck. I knew this was a bad idea.*
I looked at mum, then dad, desperately trying to read the situation; I was drawing a blank. *Shit.* Chrissy broke the silence.
"Jack was worried about what you would think, so I thought we'd just jump in head first" she said.
"Well, it's very nice to meet you" dad said "Would you like a cup of tea?"
"Love one ta" Chrissy said. Dad smiled, and retreated to the kitchen, pulling mum along with him. "Come along dear, you can get the cups ready"
Mum looked at me with a look that I couldn't quite decipher.
"See?" Chrissy said "That wasn't so bad now was

it?"

"What? It's a fucking disaster. I can't tell if mum is happy or not" I sort of half-whispered in mild panic. I really couldn't tell what was going on in mum's head.

Chrissy tried to reassure me. She took my hand and said "Hey. She is, I can tell. And that's a good sign right?"

"Guess so" I said, still pretty worried, and not at all convinced.

"Come on, let's go to the kitchen" Chrissy pulled my arm, and we went to join my parents in the kitchen.

I could hear mum talking to dad as we approached the door "Well, she seems lovely, don't you think? I'm so happy, he's been alone for too long" Dad just about had time to agree with her when we walked in. What? Was I dreaming?? If so, I didn't want to wake up.

We must have sat there for over an hour, the conversation starting slowly, and clumsily, but improved rapidly. Chrissy telling her life story, and mum embarrassing me with stories about me. It went better than I expected. Mum and Chrissy were getting on really well, and dad was giving me approving looks. This was great. This was more than great. This was fucking brilliant.

A short while later, we were stood by the front door, saying our goodbyes. We waved, and were walking down the front path, when mum called me back.

"What is it?" I asked.

She hugged me and said "She's great Jack. If she

makes you happy, she makes me happy"

"Thanks mum, she really does. I was so worried about what you would think"

"No need. I'm so very happy for you" she kissed my cheek and let me go.

I caught up with Chrissy, and she asked, "Everything ok?"

"Yeah, everything's ok"

Everything was more than ok; it was perfect.

I walked her home, said goodnight, and then walked back to mine in a daze of pure happiness.

I lay in bed for a while, going over the events of the last few hours, coming to no conclusion other than; pure, fucking brilliant.

No need for Mr Holmes tonight; I would sleep well.

And I did.

DAY 3

Wednesday, 19th of March.

I woke early, before the alarm. My head was still full of positivity. Last night had been great. Chrissy is far more confident than I am; I would never have done such a thing. But she did.

Too early for a tangent? Hey, too bad.
What's it like having a partner that is the polar opposite to you confidence wise? Is it a good thing? Does it add stress to a relationship? Here's my 2 pennies worth; as I discussed in the first book, I was a happy, confident, outgoing kind of guy before all the trouble started at home. After the divorce, I was a mere shell of my former self. I was anxious (was anxious before, but amplified now), stay-at-home, not wanting to socialise, and basically just sad/broken on the inside. With the advantages of being in the future to when this story took place, I can say that Chrissy's confidence has done us the world of good. It has made me do more, made me try more, made me get out more. It's what I needed. If it wasn't for her, I'd be a recluse by choice. What do you think? Good thing

or not? I'm not saying she drags me out against my will, by has an ability to make everything look positive, and thus making it easier for me to go. And she's a fantastic social partner; I'm socially anxious, and she knows it. She helps me and shields me when needed. It works perfectly.

Anyways, yawn, I was just waking up...

I checked my phone; messages from mum. I scrolled through and was happy to see they were all positive; she liked Chrissy. What was Chrissy short for? Had she met the kids? (Not something that came up last night). Many more questions. I told her I'd meet her in the café for a coffee later if she wanted, we could go through all her questions. Meet at 4? Sorted.

That done, I sent Chrissy a message thanking her for last night.

I got a response immediately:

Her: You're welcome. Turned out ok, I think?
Me: Had some messages from mum this morning; she likes you
Her: Yeay!
Me: I'm meeting her for a coffee later, just to talk about it and other stuff
Her: I'm sure she'd like that. And it would put your mind at rest.
Me: Yeah, it will
Her: I'm happy that it turned out ok
Me: It's a relief for sure
Her: Text me later and let me know how it went
Me: I will
Her: Have a great day, love you. X

Pause it there...

Love you.
Love you?
Holy shit.

In reality, I text back straight away: Love you too, speak later. X (my heart was pounding with nervous tension when I sent it, wondering if I'd get shot down. But I didn't)
However, let's take another moment her to analyse the impact of those 2 little words; Love. You.

I'm not going to lie, I had thought about saying it to her sooner, as, let's face it; I was totally and utterly in love with her. But... I didn't want to fuck everything up by saying it too soon and scaring her off. However, Chrissy being uber confident, probably sensed this and rescued me. When is too soon to say "I love you"? Some would argue that you know VERY early on if you're in love or not. There's a difference between being in Love and being in Lust. This relationship was definitely a Love one. Lust, let's face it, does come into it as she's fucking gorgeous, but having been burned and fucked over in the past, I was now far more mature and able to look past Lust and see Love. I love her. I lust for her, but not in a teenage boy kind of way. I fucking love her. As much as I hate to do this, my ex-wife (wow, feels weird saying that) once said something to me that I can now offer as words that fit the context perfectly: "I don't just love you; I'm *in love* with you." And that's exactly the case here. Hate to paraphrase her, hurts my pride to do so, but those words were pretty good. You have to admit.

I think you know if you love someone. Don't you? There's a difference between love and lust. We hadn't slept together, nothing more than innocent kisses in fact. And I was happy with that. I wasn't in any rush, and I don't think she was either. Not something I was comfortable discussing with her just yet...

Yeah, you know very quickly. Especially at my age; you don't fuck about. (As-in: waste time, mess around. not what you were thinking) There was just something about her; we just naturally clicked.

Like destiny. That chance encounter was meant to happen. The dog lead was meant to break. Nah, I don't believe in that stuff. I'm an Engineer. Pure coincidence. But a great coincidence.

I text the kids, told them I loved them and to have a great day, then put my phone down. Wait. I had an idea. I picked up my phone and had a brief text chat, then jumped up and got changed into my running gear. I looked out the window; weather was clear, and nice. Good day for it.

Did a bit of stretching, then walked down to the bridge. I saw her before I got there; looking gorgeous in the morning sun. She was doing some stretches, waiting for me to turn up.

"Morning you" I said

She jumped a little as I caught her off guard
"Morning you"
Hug. Kiss. She smelled fantastic.
"Ready?" I asked
"Be gentle with me"
"Don't worry, we'll go slow, break you in easy" I reassured her.
"I hope we're still talking about running" she said
I blushed. Shit. Fuck. Why? Grrrrr…
She kissed my cheek "I'm kidding. Come on, let's get going" she laughed.
I started my watch, and we trotted off down the towpath. I loved this woman.
We did a gentle 3k run. She did well, obviously; she was fit.
Different muscle group from cycling though, I warned her it would hurt the day after tomorrow.
Something to look forward to. We hugged, kissed, and said goodbye. *She smelled good, even after a 3k run* I thought. Damn.
I ran back home, showered, had breakfast, and went to work. First up; gear review on a new guitar amplifier (re-issue of a vintage one). I liked the way it was done. I liked the amp. I thought about buying one. *No! Don't need it!* I did the video proud; it was fantastic. Next… Instructional video.
7 hours later…
I looked up and realised I'd worked right through lunch, and it was indeed half past three. Shit. I was meeting mum at 4. I finished up (4 vids done!!!!) and left for the café.
I was hungry. Very hungry. I spotted mum across the road from the café chatting to someone. She

knew basically everyone in the villages.

She saw me and waved. I indicated I'd see her inside.

Tinkle.

"Sweet fucking Jesus. Look what the cat dragged in"

Yep, swearing will increase exponentially from here on.

"Hey mate" I walked over and hugged my friend.

"To what do we owe the pleasure?" he asked

"Meeting mum for a coffee"

"Fuck. Better watch my mouth"

"Yeah, you do that" I said with a laugh. "How did you get on with Ken? Everything sorted?"

"All sorted mate, thanks for hooking me up. Such a relief"

"Glad to hear it. You manage to book some time away?"

"Closed Friday, Saturday, Sunday, Monday dude."

"Holy shit."

"I know. Found a lovely place in Sicily"

"Fuck me. I meant a weekend away local or something. Sicily? Wow. Good effort."

"It's beautiful mate, overlooking the sea, quiet, nice bar and restaurant nearby, walking trails. All good" He said proudly.

"Well, I'm sure she'll love it" I said

"Oh, she does. She's off this afternoon, clothes shopping in the city. Not a hiker, so she's off buying gear"

I should add that Steve is a total outdoor person. Loves hiking, biking, etc. Willow, the opposite. But, he would turn her into an outdoor lover before she knew it.

Tinkle.

"Hello Mrs Beckett, lovely to see you" Steve fixed his hair, and stood straight.

"Hello Stephen" she walked over and hugged him "Lovely to see you. How are you doing? How's your mother?"

"I'm good thanks Mrs Beckett, mum is fine. She had a bit of a fall, but she's fine"

"Poor Karen, I'll give her a call later"

"Would you like a coffee?" Steve asked

"That would be lovely thank you Stephen" Mum walked off and found a table.

I followed but turned and flipped Steve the middle finger and a laugh.

He shook his head and said "Language Mr Beckett" loud enough for mum to hear.

"Funny Stephen. Funny" I laughed. Mum always called him by his proper name, it was quite funny.

He mouthed "Fuck you" and went to make mum's coffee.

I walked over to mum, hugged her, and we sat. "What's that all about?" she asked.

"Just Steve being Steve" I said. He's desperately trying to control his language; you know what he's like"

She laughed "He's always had a potty mouth, even as a youngster. But not in a nasty way"

"He's harmless" I said "Lovable rogue"

Speaking of which... "Here's your coffee Mrs Beckett"

"Thank you, Stephen," mum said

"Yeah, thank you Stephen" I mocked.

He flipped me the double fingers from behind mum's back and walked off.

All very childish. But funny.

Mum took a sip of her coffee, winced slightly, and added a spoon of sugar. "Always so bitter these fancy coffees" she said. "Needs a spoon of sugar to take the edge off"

"So, Jack, what did you want to talk about?" she asked

"I just wanted to have a chat following last night, and answer any questions you might have"

She nodded. "Chrissy?" she asked

"Christelle. Christelle Lenoir" I said.

"Fancy name" she smiled "Very pretty. French?"

"Her mother's side"

"You like her very much" she observed

"I'm in love mum, she's perfect"

"Nobody's perfect Jack" she observed

"I know that, but she's perfect enough. For me"

"Fair enough"

"Can I ask you a question?" I asked

"Of course you can"

"Do you miss Helen?

"Would it be wrong if I did?" she asked and sipped her coffee.

"No, I guess not"

"Good. I do miss her, its natural Jack. She was part of this family for a long time. These feelings don't just go away"

"I know"

"Do you miss her?" she asked. I was taken aback. Wtf?

"Me?"

"Yes, you"
"I did, for a bit. But now I don't even think about her" I said, honestly.
"You bore the brunt of all the badness Jack, it's natural that you don't think of her. We didn't, so it's harder for us, and will be more gradual."
She was making sense, I knew it, but it still angered me a bit.
"Don't be angry" she said, sensing my mood change "This will have no impact on how we feel towards Christelle"
"I know, it just hurts a bit" I said.
"I'm sorry if it does. And to be honest Jack, you'll never see us together, so it doesn't matter too much. I just didn't want to lie to you"
She was still making sense. Dammit.
Can I ask *you* a question??" she turned the tables. Shit.
"Yes, of course" I said. Uneasy.
"Will you be honest with me?" she looked me in the eye
"Always mum" I said earnestly.
"Ok then. Was the divorce your fault?" she asked.
Holy fuck. Even my own mother??
I composed myself.
"No mum, it was all on her. And that's the truth"
"Ok, I believe you. I'm sorry Jack, but we know nothing about what happened. I don't want to, it's enough for me to know it wasn't you." she said.
"You want me to tell you about it?" I asked
"Only if you think you need to" she said.
"I think I need to" I confessed.
I told her all about the divorce, the letters,

the solicitors, the cost, my mental health, the breakdowns, the suicide attempt, the medication, the kids, meeting Helen in the supermarket with Chrissy; all of it. It all just spilled out. I couldn't stop it.

She sat for a moment, processing all that I had just told her. The silence was uncomfortable.

Shit. I saw tears welling in her eyes.

"Mum?" I asked, "You ok?"

She leaned over and took me in her arms. "My beautiful boy, I'm so sorry" she sobbed.

"Mum, it's not your fault" I said

"I know, but I'm so sorry for what you had to go through. I had no idea" Still crying.

"Hey, mum, I'm ok" I tried to reassure her. Wasn't working. I could feel her pain. If one of my kids had told me what I just told her I'd feel the same way; I'd failed them. Knowing mum, she had probably filtered out everything I had just told her and been left with one item; Attempted suicide. Shit. I regretted telling her. I still do. That can't be easy knowledge for a parent. Not sure I'd ever want to know.

Time for a mini tangent?

You remember what I said earlier about being open and honest? Doesn't apply to all situations. This was a classic example. I should never have told my mum that I tried to kill myself. I would implore you never to do so either. Being a parent myself, I don't think I would want to know. Let me tell you why. My mum blames herself for not seeing how bad I really was. Every day since, and I mean EVERY day, she has text or called me to see how I'm doing. And we're talking 10 years later. That's how much it affected her. Like I said, I regret telling her. Every day. Should have kept that one to myself. Know your audience, tailor your confessions, etc. Engage brain before opening mouth. Think of how your words will affect whomever you're talking to. Please. You'll thank me.

So, back to the cafe. Mum. In tears. Shit. I felt like pond scum. *Nice one dickhead.* For once, inner voice, I agree with you.
"Why didn't you tell me what was going on?" still sobbing.
"Mum, I could barely process what was happening, let alone try to share that with someone" I tried explaining. "It just built up slowly, until that was the easiest way to make it all stop."
"I should have been able to tell" she said "I should have been able to see what was going on"
"No mum. No. You're not superwoman. You can't see what's going on in my head. It was a mistake. I know that now and would never do anything like that again."
"You promise?"
"I promise. I have too much to live for. The kids, Chrissy. I could never leave that behind"
"But..." she started. I knew where she was going.
"I know what you're going to say. I believed that the kids would be better off with Helen, without their failure of a father. Believed. Past tense. I don't believe that anymore."
"Ok Jack. Promise you'll talk to me in future if you have issues? I'm your mother, I will never stop

worrying about you, regardless of how old you are."

"Mum, I'm sorry. I promise I will talk to you more" I said. And I kept that promise. I speak to my mum all the time about even the silliest of issues.

"Good. Now I have to go and sort myself out. I must look a state" she said. She stood and went off to the toilet.

Steve appeared almost immediately. "What the fuck did you say? She's crying you dick"

"Yeah, I know mate. I told her about all my troubles and issues"

"Please tell me you didn't tell her about the thing?" he asked worried.

My shoulders slumped "Yes, I did. I was being open and honest"

"You stupid prick" he slapped the back of my head "The fuck you thinking?"

"Yeah alright mate" I said angrily "I'm angry enough at myself without you poking your nose in"

Hands up in defeat "Sorry Jack, I'll just leave you to it." He walked away.

FUCK SAKE!!!!! Was there anyone I wasn't going to upset today? *Yeah dickhead, nice job!* Fuck off! I checked myself. Shit. No, I hadn't said that out loud. Thank God.

My mother re-appeared; her face suitably made up. She was trying to look composed, but I could see some of the light in her eyes had dimmed. And it would stay that way forever.

I decided to try change the subject to something more cheerful, so I asked her what she thought of

Chrissy.

"She seems lovely Jack. Very confident, isn't she?"

"Yeah, but I think that's good for me. Especially nowadays"

We talked a short while longer, and then it was time for her to go and make dinner.

"Thanks mum" I said "And I'm really sorry"

"Don't worry about me. You just make sure you stay happy. Come over for dinner next Sunday. I'll do roast lamb."

"That would be perfect" I said. My mum makes a terrific roast.

"Oh. Wait. She's not a vegetarian, is she?"

"No mum, she's not. I'll ask, but I'm sure she'd love to come"

"Oh, good" she said. "Take care Jack. I love you."

"Love you too mum"

We hugged, and she left. I stood watching her walking away and could tell that she would never be the same again. Shit.

I took a breath. Now I have another relationship to save. I turned around and saw him staring at me from behind the counter. He looked furious. Fuck.

"You're a fucking prick" he said

"Deserve that. I'm sorry mate. I shouldn't have snapped at you"

"No, you fucking shouldn't have. But you know what?" he asked, still angry.

Sigh "What?"

"I forgave you straight away you tit. Come here" He held out his arms, and we hugged for a while.

I cried. I cried a lot. What is it about this guy that brings out the emotions and tears???

"You're in a good place buddy" he re-assured me "All that shit is gone now"
He was right. I was in a good place, and all that shit was gone. Fucking hell, how did he always know what to say???
"Alright, you're getting my t shirt wet now you melt. Go. Get out of here. Go home, have a beer, and reflect on how good you have it."
"You're right. Thanks man"
I grabbed my stuff and went home.

Inside I felt like a piece of shit. But, reflecting on Steve's wise words (do not tell him I said that!), I realised that I did have it good. But if I had it so good, why did I still get so low? Depression? Anxiety? I wasn't sure. I only knew my mood could change in an instant, because of the smallest thing. Didn't even have to be anything of consequence. Something tiny could send me spiralling downward into the depths of despair.
Not tonight though. Tonight, I would do exactly what Steve suggested; I would have a beer or two and play some music to keep me happy whilst thinking about Chrissy and the kids.
Nice thought dickhead, but we both know that ain't gonna happen. Shit. Inner voice was right again.
I got home, changed, curled up in bed, and cried myself to sleep. Anxiety sucks.
I'll conclude this chapter with a few lines by a famous writer* that sum it up:

They say the loneliest number is one.
But that isn't true.
It is possible to be alone,

Even when there are two.

*= Me. (Takes a bow...)

DAY 4

Thursday, 20th of March.

Almost slept through my alarm this morning. I was mentally and physically drained.

I had a full day of work ahead of me, and just couldn't face it. Today was a day where I just wanted to stay in bed all day with the curtains shut. It was almost 08.30. I should get up. *Nah, stay where you are loser!* Ugh. Yeah, you're right. *Good boy.*

I pulled the duvet over my head and went back to sleep. I was woken by someone banging on my front door. I dragged myself out of bed and went to see who it was. Steve.

"Fucking hell. I knew it. You're a state. Here" He handed me a coffee "Sit down and get that down you."

I trundled into the kitchen and sat at the table.

"I had a feeling you would crash last night. I'm sorry, I should have called"

I waved his comment away "Mate, I'm fine"

"Fuck you are. Look at you. I'll get you some breakfast" Before I could object, he was off looking

through the fridge. "Jesus man, you need to get shopping in, there's fuck all here"
He found some eggs and made me a fried egg sandwich. "Eat"
I ate. I didn't feel particularly hungry, but it smelled good. It was good. Steve knows about the effects of food and drink on the human mind, it was his craft after all. It was working; I was rising up through the darkness.
I finished the sandwich and looked at my friend. He was the perfect best friend.

Tangent.

He had always been there for me. He always knew when I was crashing. He always knew what to say. He always knew how to comfort me. He always knew when I needed space.
I realise I am extremely lucky to have someone like Steve around me. Most people likely don't. You really need someone to rely on. Someone to pick you up off the floor. Find someone, anyone. It can be hard, but please try. You need someone to talk to. Be it a parent, sibling, relative, work colleague. Find someone. You need it.

"Better?"
"Yes mate"
"Good. You going to be ok? I've left Willow on her own and I really need to get back"
"Go, I'm good mate"
We hugged, and Steve left. "Text or call me if you need to" he said as he left.
I closed the door, promising to do so, and took a

deep breath. And…relax.
Get dressed, do a run. Go. Now! Ok, ok. I went and put my running gear on and did 6k on the treadmill. It worked; felt great after.
I showered, dressed, and checked my phone. Shit. Message from Helen. (Yes, she had unblocked me) Could I have the kids from tonight as she forgot she had theatre tickets for a play in London? She was taking her mum. Hmm. That was supposed to be me. I paid for those, I thought. Nope, leave it Jack.
There was still a lot to do. I had 5 videos left to edit this week, which would take most of today, and a bit of tomorrow. I needed to get stuck in.
The kids are coming this evening, and I needed to go shopping first. Or, I could take them with me when they got here. We could get some fresh pizzas and watch a movie. Sorted.
Ok, now get to work. Yes Sir!

I had a few messages throughout the morning form my mum, Chrissy, and the kids. Mum checking if I was ok. (Would repeat every day for the next 10+ years), Chrissy also checking if I was ok. Did the world think I was fragile and doomed? Shit. That wasn't the image I wanted to project. I responded truthfully; I was not ok, but Steve had been round and picked me up.
The kids (both) asked if Chrissy was coming over for pizza too. I hadn't even thought to ask her. *Oh. Well done Jack, she'll feel properly included now...* Shut up already. I text her and asked. She was free from 4, so would come straight over. I said we'd

meet in the café as I wanted to say bye to Steve and Willow as they were going away for a long weekend. Deal.

I stopped for lunch, and to check the post. Letter from her solicitor. Shit. I stared at it for a bit. What now? Surely everything was settled and agreed?
Fearing the worst, I opened it. Please be good, please be good I thought. It was ok. Just a letter confirming that all the financial agreements had been met, and that the direct debit for child support had been verified. Basically: Hi Jack, just to let you know you've got a new 25 year mortgage to pay for the equity you so generously gave to Helen, and you're going to be skint for the rest of your life. Genius. Thanks legal system. Another job well done. Here's a woman that didn't pay a penny towards the mortgage ever, but apparently is entitled to half the equity. Someone explain that to me without bullshitting. Yeah, didn't think so.

Anyway. Done. Don't let it get to you. I filed the letter and made myself a sandwich. I text Steve to let him know I was ok, and that we'd be at the caff around 4. Thumbs up response.
I got back to work, and managed to finish all but 2 videos by half three. Sent off all finished work, and ran around the house making sure it was ready for the kids.
All done, I made my way to the café. Chrissy was already there when I walked in. She was stood chatting to Willow about the holiday. They both seemed equally excited, whilst Steve stood off to the side watching them with a smile.

"Hey bud" I said, walking over to him.
"Hey Jack, you good?"
"Yeah, all good. Thank you mate, I really appreciate you being there for me."
"Ach, you've done the same for me, it's what we do."
"You ready for the holiday?" I asked
"Yeah, I have packed my few things in that" he pointed to a small holdall. "Whilst Willow is taking that" pointing to a large suitcase.
"Ah. Yeah, best get used to that mate, girls don't travel light" I laughed.
"Whatever. Doesn't really bother me. Just look at how happy she is" he nodded in Willow's direction. "Thanks for suggesting it, I was too blind to see it"
I hugged him and said "Hey, just go have a great time"
"Oh don't you worry mate, I will" he winked. Smooth. "You text me if you need to ok?" he said seriously.
"Yeah, I will"
I called over to Willow "Hey Willow, have a great time, and look after this lump would you?"
"Oh I will Jack, don't you worry"
"Yeah, have a brilliant time, don't forget I want to see plenty of pictures" Chrissy added and hugged both of them. "Have a great time guys"
We said our goodbyes, and left them to close up. I was happy for them both, but mostly for my friend; he deserved someone good. And Willow was good for him.
"I'm so jealous" Chrissy said as we walked back to

mine

"Yeah, must be nice" I said

"When was the last time you had a holiday?" she asked me

"Well, we took the kids to Legoland last year, and had a week in the Lake District"

"You didn't go abroad?"

"Difficult. Well, not difficult, just expensive. Travelling in school holidays is ridiculously expensive"

"Ah yeah, I forgot about that" she said

"We took them to France the year before. Tended to go abroad every other year" I added

"And this year?" she asked coyly.

"Well, we had planned to go to Greece somewhere for a week, but that's died a death"

"You could still take them yourself though couldn't you?" she asked

"Hmmmm. Bit difficult with the finances now. I'll have to see"

"You're forgetting something" she noted

"Oh?" What did I miss?

"You have a partner that earns a great wage. If she was allowed to join that is"

"You would want that?" I asked stupidly.

"Are you kidding? Two weeks on a Greek island? Sun, tavernas, Greek food?"

"One week" I corrected

"No Jack, two weeks" she winked "Let me help make it happen"

"Are you sure?" I asked

"Jack, I've just sold my flat, and I am, was, alone. Trust me, I have money saved"

"Only if you're sure" I added
"I'm sure. Let's plan it." She hugged and kissed me. "I'm looking forward to it already" she said excitedly.
"Ok, let's do it" I said.

Mini Tangent.

Holiday together?? Was this too much too soon? Believe me when I say it wasn't about the money. I didn't have an issue with her paying towards the holiday. It was more that I thought it was maybe too soon. What do you think? This thought process was obviously processed very quickly given the conversation above. I did agree, and I was happy with it, but there was that little niggle in my mind that the kids would maybe think it was too early. And especially people looking on from the outside. And, what would Helen think? *Who cares dickhead!* Yeah, like Chrissy said; I shouldn't care about "Other people". It's what we thought that mattered. Ok, done.

We got to the house, picked up the car, and drove out to the bus stop to wait for the kids. We were a bit early, so Chrissy spent the time buried in her phone whilst I took in the world outside.
"Are you looking at places to go already?" I joked
"Of course" she said "Gotta book early"
I was kidding. Jesus. She didn't waste time.
"You want quiet, like a villa with pool? Or just a hotel?" she asked
"What do you think?" I said mockingly.
"Villa it is. Leave it to me, I'll find something the

kids will love"

I spent a moment just watching her. She was gorgeous, and looked so happy. I was lucky. *Yeah you are. Punching well above your weight Jacko.* Oddly enough, I agree. I was. I am. Just look at her; pretty, successful, confident, positive, and she loved the kids. And loved me. This perfect woman sat next to me loved *me*. Me, with all my flaws and history and emotional baggage. What was she thinking? Was she some sort of angel, sent to rescue me?

To this day, I still think the same. That gorgeous woman is now my wife, and very proud to be so. She'll tell anyone that. It embarrasses me and makes me happy at the same time. She's just perfection in female form. And she's mine. Everyone tells me how lucky I am, and I totally agree with them each time. Still don't see what she sees in me, but I guess that's just one of life's little mysteries.

Eventually, I was broken from my daydream by James bashing on the windscreen. "Hey dad! Wake up!"
"Hey buddy" I smiled. I got out and hugs my kids tightly. "Good to see you guys, I missed you so much"
"Miss you too dad" Elsie said before casting me aside. "Hi Chrissy, how are you?" Ah I see, been ditched for someone better already! Good to see. It made me happy that she had bonded with Chrissy so well.
"I am good thank you. Hope you're ready to do

my hair tonight, it needs a bit of loving" she said, rustling her already perfect looking hair. Elsie clapped her hands excitedly." Yeay! Yeah, I brought my stuff" she said, patting her bag, and jumped in the back.

"Hi James" Chrissy said to James "You ok?"

"Hi, yeah I'm good thanks" he responded shyly and joined his sister in the back of the car. That's funny, I thought with a smile. My confident boy reduced to shyness by a beautiful woman. Couldn't blame him though, remembering what he had said; *She's tidy dad, well done*. I rolled my eyes and started the car.

Elsie spent the entire car journey there and back chatting excitedly about school and her friends.

No awkward run-ins at Sainsbury's this time; we walked around and filled the trolley with what we needed for the weekend. And a lot more besides.

We got back home, and I at least got the kids to help bring the shopping in before they disappeared. James to the PlayStation, and Elsie to her room to chat to her friends. Kids. Beautiful.

I was putting away the shopping whilst Chrissy was glued to her phone, and making notes on a pad. "You're not getting your hair done?" I asked.

"I promised her we'd do it after dinner" she responded.

"I thought we were watching a movie after dinner?" I asked

"Jack, look at her, she's super excited. The movie will have to wait" she laughed.

She was right. It was more important that they

bonded. We could watch a movie anytime. I wasn't expecting James to do so either; he had his headset on, about to commando raid a building or something with his friends online. He'd be lost there all night. How things have changed since I was young.

The ovens were warming up. I got myself a beer form the fridge, and offered Chrissy one. "Yes please, something dark" I handed her a Stout and a glass. "Ooh, thanks". I looked at the pad, and saw that she had a list of about 10 places already. Oh, and her handwriting was beautiful. She was left-handed, but not in an awkward way; her handwriting was very flowy and arty; lots of bows and swirls. Not important, but just something I picked up on. I snapped out of it, and put pizzas in the ovens. "20 minutes guys!" I shouted. No response, but I know they heard me.

I went up and checked my emails quickly. One comment from client, very small change. Happy.

The ovens beeping told me dinner was ready. I knocked on Elsie's door, and gave James a prod.

A few minutes later, they showed up; the smell of pizza too tempting.

"Hey guys. I have some news" I said as we sat eating
"What's up?" James asked, only half interested.
"We're going on holiday this year, probably to Greece"
"Yeah!" James shouted "Result!"
Elsie looked unsure. "What's up Ello?"
"Daddy, is Chrissy coming?" she asked
"Do you want her to come?" I asked, looking at

Chrissy for support.

"Yes, I do" she said confidently.

"I'd love to come" Chrissy added "Thank you" she winked at Elsie.

Smiles all round. I was proud of my brood.

We spent the rest of dinner talking about where we could go. James didn't mind as long as there was a pool, Elsie just wanted to be near the beach. "I think we can do all of that" Chrissy told them

"It's going to be epic!" James said smiling. "I can't wait"

"Me neither buddy. Gonna be great." I said, eating my last slice.

After dinner, the kids retreated to their respective lairs to do whatever kids did. We got another beer each and crashed on the sofa. Content. "No hair tonight?" I asked

"Nope, she's probably excited about the holiday"

Probably was. Content, I put my beer down, and said "Right, Lenoir, let me see what you've got"

"Mr Beckett! How very forward of you" she said, feigning shock.

"The list. Show me the list" I rolled my eyes.

"That's ok then, I'm not *nearly* that easy" she winked.

We spent some time looking at the places on her list, whittling it down to a top 3; One on Skopelos, One on Corfu, and the last on Santorini. They were all great, and the kids would love any of them.

"You think the kids would like them?" she asked

"Are you kidding? They'd love any of those"

"Shall we let them choose?" she asked "Might be nice?"

"Yeah, we'll ask them over dinner tomorrow" I said "If you're coming for dinner tomorrow?"
"Of course I will, I'd love to" She kissed me and continued "But now, I'll have to go home"
"Yeah you do" I said "Another one of those and I wouldn't trust myself" I said nodding at my beer.
"Oo-er!" she said "Easy tiger". Shit. Shit. Shit. Shit. Shit. What the fuck did I just say????
"Bye guys!" she shouted upstairs as we walked past. "Bye Chrissy!" from Elsie. Silence from James. "He's probably wearing his headset" I explained.
"Ah, I see. Well, thank you for a lovely evening Jack Beckett" she said, taking me in her arms
"Thank you for your wonderful company Christelle Lenoir" I responded.
We kissed. It got a bit longer each time I noticed. Not that I was complaining.
My god, she smells good.
I got her coat, and saw her to the door "See you tomorrow?"
"Yeah, I'll be here for about half 5 if that's ok? Got a bit of work on tomorrow"
"Perfect" I said. We kissed again and said goodbye. I closed the door with a contented sigh. *I love her*. I thought, *I love her so much*.

"Guys, its 8 o'clock!" I shouted "Time for bed! School tomorrow!"
Usual moans and complaints, with eventual surrender. Eventually they both came down to say goodnight. "Goodnight, guys, love you both" I kissed them both on the head, and they ran off upstairs. "Don't be on your phones too long!" I

shouted after them.

I went up and made the requested change to the client's video and sent it back to them. Done.
Surfed the web for a bit, looking at flights to all three places on the shortlist, also looked at car hire & things to do etc. Before I knew it, it was almost midnight. Shit. I shutdown, brushed my teeth, and went to bed.

I listened to a bit of Sherlock and fell asleep a happy man.

DAY 5

Friday, 21st of March.

Up early to sort the kid's breakfast & lunches out. They were uber tired, and just about made it to the bus stop in time. I already had my running kit on, so went for a nice run in the early morning sun. It was fantastic; the air was clear, the sky blue. Just idyllic. Had a shower, made myself a bit of breakfast, and went to work. I wanted to get this done by lunchtime. Don't know why. I had nothing planned after. The cafe was shut, Chrissy was working, and my parents had gone up to see dad's sister in Peterborough. Oh well, I'll worry about that after I've finished. Let's go Jackie boy.

I flashed up my pc and laptop and settled down to work. Scrolled though what I had left and decided to start with a song review. Not heard of the artist, but the music was actually pretty good. That video took me about 2 hours to finish, and I sent it off straight away. 2 left. Gear review or melodic soloing instructional? Hmm.... Instructional. Did my usual; watched the raw footage right through a couple of times whilst making notes. Then did my editing magic. Done. Sounds simple, but still took almost 2.5 hours to complete. Finished product looked pretty good so I was happy. Sent it off. Last one. Let's get it done. Finally finished just after 1300. Bit later than I would have liked. Only left me a few hours before the kids would be home. What to do? I text Chrissy but got no response; she was probably busy. Hmm.... Bored.

Checked phone. Message from Steve, letting me know they got there ok, and a picture of them at a beautiful beach. Bastard. I told him as much. Still no reply from Chrissy. *Ha! Your little comment last night really fucked you up!* No, it hadn't. She was just busy. *Or you put her off you fucking pervert.* "Will you fuck off!" I shouted. *Lol! That's the second time you've shouted at nobody you fucking nutjob!* I needed to get out! I grabbed my coat and went out for a walk. Didn't know where to, just anywhere. It was cold and I was feeling it. Soon enough, I found myself shaking with cold. Jesus, what the hell is wrong with me?? I found a bench near the bridge and sat. I must have sat there for almost an hour. Just staring. I was so cold, but I didn't want to go home, and I had nowhere else to go. I started crying. Fuck. I'm lost. I got my phone out and tried calling Chrissy. Thankfully, she answered.

"Hey you, you ok?" she asked. I couldn't speak; I just cried. "Jesus Jack, where are you? Are you home?" she sounded panicky. "Hello??"

"I'm by the bridge" I managed. I sounded like shit, even to myself.

"Stay there, I'm coming. Just stay where you are, ok?" she called off

I dropped my phone and just sat there, staring at it. I couldn't feel my hands. I was a mess.

Chrissy came running over a few minutes later "Jesus Jack, Jesus, are you ok??" she sat next to me and picked me up. "Hey, are you ok?" she said holding my face in her hands "You're freezing! Where's your coat?" she asked.

My coat? I was wearing it. Wasn't I? *And...You're officially fucked in the head.*

"What are you doing out here? Why didn't you call me sooner? Come on, I need to get you warm"

She picked up my phone, then stood me up and supported me as we walked back to my house. She got the key from my pocket, and opened the door. "In here" she led me to the sofa, and lay me down. "I'll be right back" she rushed off upstairs and came back with a duvet. "Here, get warm in this" she said, wrapping me in it. I was shivering, and just couldn't speak. I wanted to, but my brain wouldn't let me. "My god Jack, what happened?" she asked, but I couldn't answer. She took the duvet off, and lay down under it with me. "Here. Come here" she said, and she cradled my head on her chest. "You poor thing. What happened?" she was crying. I felt like shit. I had let her down. I had let everyone down. But I still couldn't speak. Why couldn't I speak??? "Shhhh. Shhh, it's going to be ok. It's going to be ok" she said, comforting me.

I could feel the warmth slowly coming back into

my body. My tears had dried up; I had nothing left. I just slept. I don't know how long we lay there, but it wasn't for more than half an hour or so. I woke, and she was still stroking my head. "Hey, are you ok? You scared the shit out of me"

"I'm sorry" I said. *Weak Jack! Weak!* "I don't know what happened"

"I found you sat on the bench in the freezing cold without a coat on. What were you doing there?"

"I went out for a walk. I wasn't feeling so good. I thought I put my coat on"

"No, you didn't. Jesus, I don't know what to do. What do I do Jack?" She was upset.

"I'm so sorry. I can't explain. I had a good morning, then I thought I just went out for a walk because I was bored"

"You need to promise me something" she said

"What?"

"Promise me you'll take your medication every time you start feeling down. And we need to find you some help"

"No, I don't want a head doctor" I said vehemently.

"Not a head doctor Jack, just a counsellor, someone to talk to"

I sat up. "You think I need to?" I asked

"Jack, you were sat on a bench in minus 2 degrees without a coat. Yes, you need to"

She had a point. What the fuck had happened today? Was I finally losing it? *Heheheheh....*

"Ok. I'll find someone" I said.

"Promise me"

"I promise"
"I was fucking scared" she punched my shoulder.
"Ouch!"
"You deserve that. Don't scare me like that again"
"I'm really sorry" I said. Again.
"You ok now? Bit better?"
"Yeas thanks. I am."
"Good. Go get a shower and change, your kids will be here in a bit. I'm sure you wouldn't want them to see you like this"
"No, I do not" I said, and went off to have a shower. Chrissy tidied away the duvet and went to make me a mug of tea.
I finished, dressed, and went down. "I'm so sorry Chrissy" I said. *Again, you moron!* "I don't know what happened"
"You're hurt. Here" she pointed at my heart "and you're hurt here" pointed at my head. "We need to get you better. I can help with the here (heart), but not so much the here (head)".
"I promise I'll find someone to talk to. I can see that I need help." And I did. I was a mess. Shit.
"Good. And don't go worrying about me running away scared. I'm here to stay" she re-assured me.
"I love you" I said.
"I love you too, you nutter"
"I'm so ashamed" I said, hanging my head.
"Of what? Being human? Jack, just because you're a man doesn't mean you're immune to emotional damage."

Let's stop it there and talk about that for a little.

As men, we're often thought of as cold, not caring, able to move on after something like a divorce. It's amazing how people think that men will just walk away from their children without a care in the world. Or from their ex for that matter (If the divorce isn't their fault). *"He'll be shacked up with someone else before you know it"* How many times have you heard that one? It's not true. I was DEVASTATED when I got divorced. Not seeing my kids everyday almost killed me. It was terrible, the worst period of my life. And the darkest. The highlight of my day was coming home from work and the kids would run out with smiley faces to greet me.

Coming home to an empty house is soul destroying. It really is. You basically just exist. The house is immaculate or a total mess, depending on what kind of person you are. Mine was always spotless. Cleaning kept my mind occupied.

The wrong thing to do is to allow yourself to enter the cave of self-pity. That's not good. Make sure you have something to do, and exercise. Exercise is good for the mind. Any form of exercise; go for a walk, run, cycle, whatever. It helps, trust me.

What I'm basically trying to say is that men ARE susceptible to emotional damage. We are. You are. Crying helps. It does. It's a great release. Just let yourself go sometime. I used to do it a lot, almost every night in bed. Because that's the worst time;

in bed. Alone. In the dark. With just your thoughts. Buy headphones, subscribe to some audio book app or other, listen to podcasts, or listen to music. Anything to help your mind stay on track. It does work. Well, it did for me. Still does. If my mind is racing at a million miles an hour, I put my headphones in and have a bedtime playlist I listen to. My wife knows to just leave me to it. And that's another important thing, but I'll go into that a bit later.

Back to Jack (lol)....

"We need to get this fixed" she kissed my forehead. My god she smells nice I thought. She really did. And still does.

She put the pack of tablets on the table "take one of these and keep them close all the time" I did as I was told.

"You have 20 minutes or so till the kids get here. You going to be ok? I have to get back and finish some stuff. I just ran out and left it"

"I'll be fine. You go" I hugged her tight "Thank you"

"No need. That's why I'm here. See you in an hour or so" she kissed me and left me to it.

I sat at the kitchen table wondering what the hell I had just done to her. Are you insane? *Yep, you are buddy.* No, I'm not. I'm just damaged. Shrug it off.

I did. I went to the front room and picked up my go-to minidisc containing my favourite happy song; Just a Day by Feeder. I pressed play, the effect was immediate; I jumped around like a lunatic and

enjoyed the few minutes of pure, unadulterated joy it gave me. (Try it)
Now I was in a good place. Tablet may have been helping that, but I didn't care. I was good.

Kids showed up a few minutes later, and the house was instantly alive. I hugged them close and told them I loved them. My world was complete. We ate pasta, and talked about their day in school, and they had plenty of questions about the holiday. I told them we would talk about the holiday when Chrissy got here in a bit.
She showed up just in time for ice cream.
"Hey" I said smiling.
"Hey you. You ok?"
"Yeah, I'm good. So, the kids have a few questions about the holiday...."
"Oh really?" Chrissy turned to the kids, and they started bombarding her with questions.
"Whoa! Whoa! Hey, we have had a look, and have a shortlist of 3 places" she pulled out a tablet, and brought up the 3 villas we'd chosen. "Have a look at these, and choose one"
The kids took the tablet and disappeared into the living room.
"Wow, they're keen" she said
"It's been a while since we went abroad, they miss it"
"Well, we shall have to make it a holiday to remember" she said, her enthusiasm showing.
"Just a plane ride anywhere will make it a holiday

to remember for those two" I said jokingly

"It's going to be so great; I'm really looking forward to it"

"Me too" I smiled.

We were about to kiss, when the kids came running back in "We have chosen!" shouted Elsie

"Ooh hello. Ok, what's the verdict?" I said

"We have chosen..." Elsie started, then looked at James, who finished "Skopelos"

"Nice choice"

Elsie chimed up "We chose it because we've never heard of it"

"And it has a great pool" James added.

"Well, Skopelos it is. And you know what else?" Chrissy asked

"What?" they both said

"Skopelos comes with an extra bonus!"

"It does?" I asked, confused.

"Yes. You can't fly to Skopelos, you have to fly to Skiathos and get a ferry"

"Ooh, a ferry ride too!" Elsie said excited

"Not just a Ferry ride, we're going to spend a few days on Skiathos too" Chrissy said waving her hands in the air enthusiastically.

"Get in!" James said

Elsie was already looking up Skiathos on the tablet, silly with excitement.

"We are?" I asked

"Yes, we are. I found a 2-centre deal, which gives us a villa on Skiathos for 4 days, then Skopelos for ten days."

"You did?"
"Yep, found it last night" she said proudly
"You're a miracle" I said, squeezing her hand.
"Oh I know" she replied smugly.
"And it gets better" she added with a wink
The kids both looked up from the tablet
"We're going on a boat trip to spend the day in Athens. We get to see all the cool sights"
"Yeah!" the kids were reaching insanity level excitement.
"You organised all this already?" I asked
"Nope, but I researched it all, just got to book" She replied proudly.
"Wow." I said. "That's great"
"Hey, are you ok with it? I mean, I didn't mean to do all this without you, I just did it all last night."
"No, I don't have a problem with it at all" I said honestly "I'm just amazed at how good you are"
"You ain't seen nothing yet Beckett" she replied with a wink.
Wow. This woman is perfect. I thought to myself. What the hell does someone like her see in damaged goods like me? *Erm, nope. Let's not do that. Just be happy.* I am. She makes me happy. I love her. I really do.

"Right. You two" I said pointing at my kids "Dishes & clean-up"
"Dad!"
"No moans. You do it, you get PlayStation till ten James, Elsie you get to keep your phone."

Done deal. No complaints. Didn't expect any.
Chrissy went and got a couple of beers from the fridge, then motioned at me to follow her into the living room.
"What's up?" I asked
"Have a seat"
I sat, slightly concerned
"Here's what's going to happen Jack Beckett. You are going to let me pay for this holiday. No protests." she said earnestly
"But…" I started
She held up a finger "Hey. I said no protests."
"Ok"
"Don't think for a second that you won't be doing something for me in return" she added
"Oh?" I said with a raised eyebrow
"You, Sir, are taking *me* to Florence for a week. Just you and me"
"Florence?"
"No questions. You just are."
Hey, I didn't mind that at all; I loved Italy. The food, the people, the sights.
"Deal" I said, and we shook hands.
"Good. Not like you had much of a choice anyway" she winked and kissed me.

Was I dreaming? Did I wake up on a different planet today? Could my life possibly be this perfect?
What the hell was going on? How did I meet someone this perfect? She was very confident &

all the things I was basically not, but I loved that about her.

"Can I ask you a question now?" I asked
"Shoot" she said, taking a sip of her beer.
"When is your birthday?"
"17 August. Why?"
"No reason, just realised I didn't know"
"Yours?" she asked in return
"11 November"
"Armistice day baby"
"Yep, difficult to forget"
"Three months older than me" she smiled
"Could be worse" I mocked
"True, you could be far older"
"I was thinking far younger" I joked. This resulted in another shoulder punch
"Ouch!"
"Definitely deserved that" she said.
We finished our beers, and it was time for her to go home
"I wish you didn't have to go" I said
"Steady on Mr Beckett. I'm going to sit with my aunt for a bit, she misses my company"
"My loss" I said sadly
"Soon enough my love, soon enough" She kissed me, and went off to say bye to the kids.
We said our goodbyes, and she left, with promises of coming back tomorrow. "I have to, I'm getting my hair done" she winked.
Another great evening. *Will it be like this forever?* I

thought. I didn't know, but certainly hoped so.

I got myself another beer and watched some tv. I'd completely neglected Jack Bauer, but wasn't really in the mood for it tonight, so watched an episode of Sherlock instead.

After it had finished, I cleared up, and went up to say goodnight to my children. They were both so happy. Elsie was particularly excited about doing Chrissy's hair tomorrow.

I kissed them both goodnight & went to bed myself. It had been a hell of a day. One I hoped never to repeat. Well, just the bad parts. The good parts would live in my mind forever.

Sherlocked out, I listened to some music instead.

I think I lasted 2 songs before falling into a deep sleep.

DAY 6

Saturday, 22nd of March.

Ugh. Struggle to open my eyes. I slowly became more conscious of my surroundings; noise of the kids chattering away downstairs, brightness of sun coming through the curtains. I felt like I had the handover from hell. But I didn't, I was just exhausted. Mentally exhausted. I looked at the alarm clock; 0915. Jesus. Next to it was a mug of coffee. I reached out and took a sip. Lukewarm. James had probably made it for me an hour ago or so. Bless him. I drank it all. Not because I felt obliged to, but because I needed it. I sat up and looked at my phone. Messages from Steve with more awesome pictures. My mum asking if I was ok, and if they could come over today. Chrissy checking on how I was. I responded to all and got up. No running this morning, maybe later. I text Chrissy quickly and told her to bring her running gear. Then I opened the curtains and the window. I took in a few deep breaths of fresh cold air. Felt good. The day was off to a good start.

Downstairs, the kids were video calling Helen, so I closed the living room door over to give them privacy. Made my way to the kitchen to fix a fresh coffee. Cat jumped up on the side and started head-butting me. "You want food? Come on then" Cat dutifully followed me out and sat by her bowl whilst I put some food in it for her. "Good cat" I stroked her as she ate. Went back into the kitchen, and put the radio on. Ugh, James had been at it; radio bloody one. I changed it to my preferred station, sat at the table, and sipped my coffee. Didn't need breakfast, just sat there listening to the sounds of the house, and thinking about Chrissy. I'd met her, what, about 3 weeks ago?

Look at how far we'd come already:

- She'd seen me at my absolute worst, and was ok with it
- We'd planned a family holiday
- We'd said "I love you" to each other.
- She'd met my kids
- My kids loved her. James thinks she's "tidy" (ok....) and Elsie who just loves everything about her. (especially her hair)

So I know what you're thinking, and naturally so:

- When are you going to sleep with her?

Let me explain. First of all; none of your business. This really isn't that kind of book. Second, I wasn't ready. That might sound weird, but look at where my mental health is at. I've just come out of a long relationship, separated from my kids, struggling with the financial implications. I had a lot on my plate. Believe me, sex was the furthest thing from my mind. I'm not going to lie; Chrissy is fit. Like really gorgeous. Totally my type. If I was in the right frame of mind, things might be different. But in this case, I think my state of mind was playing in my favour. Things were going slow. No pressure. Everything was happening organically. We hadn't even talked about being intimate. I was getting no signals form Chrissy that she was in a mad rush to jump into bed. And I hope she was getting the same from me. It would happen. It will happen. Speaking from the future context; it did happen.

And it was great when it did. But that's not going to be in this book as it wasn't in the next couple of weeks. Hint; we were in Florence. Anyway, that's the elephant in the room dealt with. Sorry to disappoint. No steamy scenes in this book.

The kids had finished talking to their mother and came into sit with me. "Morning guys, sorry I slept in"
"No worries dad" James said. Elsie just hugged me and asked, "When is Chrissy coming?"
"Wow, no good morning dad? Just, when's Chrissy coming?" I said, ruffling her hair "Stop!" she laughed. "I just wanted to know is all"
"I don't know Ello, maybe a bit later on. I haven't asked."
"Can you? Pleeeeeeeease?"
"Ok, Ok" I picked up my phone and text her. She replied a few seconds later: 10 ish ok?
"Yeay!" Elsie exclaimed and ran off upstairs to get ready.
"Can I go see Sean today dad?" James asked

"Sure mate, just text me if you go off out anywhere ok?"
"No worries, thanks dad. I'll be home around lunch" He ran off to get dressed, texting his best mate as he went.
"Looks like I'm going to be on my own today then" I said to no-one in particular. Elsie would be busy doing Chrissy's hair for a few hours, so I had some time to fill. *Your parents are coming dumbass.* Ah yeah, so they were. Thanks, inner voice. For once. I went off and had a shower & got dressed. By the time I came back down, James had already left, and Elsie was sat in the living room watching tv, patiently waiting. My parents were coming at about 11. That gave me an idea; I could take Chrissy out for a few beers and a bite to eat in the George. We could have a bit of "us" time. Yes, we had plenty of "us" time during the week, but I was generally in a better, happier place mentally when the kids were here. So, this would work perfectly; we could have a laugh, chat about the holiday, talk about each other, us. Great. Smile.

I went and sat next to Ello on the sofa. She was watching some bizarre Japanese style cartoon garbage, but I just wanted to sit with her. She snuggled in, and I kissed the top of her head. "You hungry Ello?" I asked
"No, I'm ok. James made us some toast"
"Good. Just checking"
We sat in silence; her enjoying whatever rubbish

she was watching. Me, just enjoying being with my daughter. Good times.

The magic was broken by the ringing of the doorbell. "You want to go see who that is?" I asked, winking at her.

She sprinted out of the room, and I could hear her excited cries when she opened the door; it was Chrissy. What a wonderful moment.

I got up and walked out to meet them. "Hey, you" I said, giving Chrissy a hug

"Morning. You good?" she asked.

"I'm more than good" It was true. I was in a fantastic mood, and equally fantastic place mentally.

"That's good. I'm off to have my hair done it seems" she said apologetically "Could you get me a coffee please?" Smile.

"Sure. Sorry, she's "Like suuuuper excited and stuff" this morning" I said.

They both disappeared off upstairs. I dutifully made Chrissy a coffee and took it up for her.

I caught a smile from Chrissy in the mirror where Elsie was busy fussing around with her hair and chattering away. "Here you go Madame" I said, putting the coffee down "Anything else I can get for you?"

"Well, not going to lie; I could do with some toast?" she said, "If you don't mind?"

"Toast, coming right up. Marmalade, honey, jam?"

"Honey please"

"Certainly, be but a moment Madame" I bowed and

walked back downstairs, smiling contentedly.
I took Chrissy's toast up and retreated to my office. Checked emails; all happy. Lots of thanks and praise. Good. Last thing I needed today was negativity. Went online quickly and ordered a couple of decent tablets. I didn't have one and saw how handy they were for the kids. They would stay here obviously. *Wait, what you being so petty for Jack? Starting that shit already? Just let them take them home with them.* WOW. Stop there for a sec. They could take them back to *their mother's place*. THIS was their home. *Yeah ok, I'll give you that one...*

Hey, just as an interesting aside; have noticed how the use of bad language has dropped since Steve went on holiday? Just came to mind as I was typing the word *shit* above. Random. Oh, but wait, there's something else that requires mild swearing:

Wait a sec Jackie boy. You buying your kids expensive gifts to score points over their mother? You starting that shit already too?
No. No I wasn't. I was just being a good dad. So, fuck right off. Prick.

There. Done.

Anyhoo…. Time for the parents to enter stage left:

Doorbell Rings

I walked over and opened the door. "You know you can just walk in right mum?" I said.

"I know, but I never will" she responded with a smile and hugged me. "How are you son?"
"I'm good thanks mum"
"Hey dad" hug.
"Hi son, good to see you"
"Coffee, Tea?" I asked as they hung their coats up
"Tea please" dad said. Mum indicated the same.
I put the kettle on and got the teapot ready.
"Kids in?" dad asked
"Well, James has gone out to see Sean for a while, he'll be back around lunchtime, and Elsie is upstairs styling Chrissy's hair"
"I'll go surprise her" dad said and went upstairs. Elsie was grandads little girl, the apple of his eye. He loved them both, but he had a soft spot for my little girl.
Mum stayed behind "I'll be right up" And came to sit next to me. "You sure you're ok?" she asked "You look tired"
"I had a bad spell yesterday mum, but I'm ok now. I keep forgetting I have pills"
"Well, you should only take those when you need to" she added. She shared my dislike of medication. "I'm glad you're ok"
She got up and followed dad upstairs to Salon Elsie. I saw to the tea, and it was poured ready for when they came back down.
"Well, she's doing a great job up there" mum said "Proper hairstylist"
"I'm not sure Chrissy would agree" dad laughed
"Ach, the girl is trying Joe" mum said.

"I'm sure she'll be happy with whatever the result is guys" I said. "Tea's poured"

We sat and chatted for a bit, then mum went off to inspect the garden whilst I helped dad sort an issue with his online banking app. Once mum had given me her usual dressing down for not caring about the garden, Chrissy and Elsie appeared.

"What do you think" Chrissy said, modelling her hair.

"It looks good, surprisingly good." I said

"Hey!" Elsie objected

"It looks great Ello. Fabulous job"

"Thank you" broad smile.

"Well, doesn't she look gorgeous Joe?" mum said

"Yes, very pretty. Well done my girl" he said, hugging Elsie

"Aaaaaagh! Grandad!" she laughed.

"Seen as you're all dolled up, do you fancy dinner at the George tonight?" I asked.

"Well, there's an invite a girl can't refuse" she said, flashing her eyelashes.

"We'll mind the kids" mum added "Love to spend time with my darlings"

"Can we order pizza?" Elsie asked. It was a grandparent tradition, they always oared I pizza if they babysat.

"Of course we can" dad said "And maybe some of that ice cream you like too

"Ooh, yeah"

I turned to mum and said "You sure you don't mind, bit short notice"

Nonsense, we'd love to. You go have a nice meal"
"Thanks mum" I said.
"How about we take a walk to the shop and see if they have your ice cream?" mum asked Elsie
"Ok, I'll get my coat" Elsie said, and ran off, grandparents in tow.
After they had left, I made Chrissy a coffee, and we sat at the table.
"You like?" she said, indicating her hair.
"I like" I said. "You look stunning". I meant it and said it in a way that communicated that.
"You say all the right things Jack Beckett" she replied
"I just speak the truth" I said "It's fairly easy with you"
She leaned over and kissed me. "I love that about you" she said. "Please never stop"
"Oh, I won't" I promised. And I stuck to my promise. Still do.
"The George, eh? You know how to spoil a girl" she said, changing the subject artfully.
"Well, it was a spur of the moment thing, and I thought it would be difficult to get in anywhere in the city on a Saturday night without booking"
"I'm kidding. You can take me anywhere and I'd be happy. I just want to be with you."
"You say all the right things Miss Lenoir." I said with a cheeky smile
I just speak the truth. It's easy with you"
I leaned over and kissed her. "I love that about you. Please never stop"

"Oh, I won't" she promised. And she stuck to her promise. Still does.
Punch to the shoulder "I see what you did there Mr Beckett, you are very cheeky"
"Ouch." I protested.
"Let me kiss that better for you" she winked.
We kissed. It was awesome. Better than awesome.
"My God you smell nice" I said. Don't know why, it just came out.
"I do?" she said, questioningly.
"Yes. You smell fantastic. Always"
"Thank you" she blushed. There it was again! As confident as she was/is, I can always make her blush with the right compliment.
"I'm guessing you wouldn't want to mess up your hair by going for a run, so fancy a walk instead?" I asked.
"Yes please, it's gorgeous out"
We got our coats (me for real this time) and headed out.

We walked over the bridge, and headed towards Steve's house. "Where we going?" Chrissy asked
"I promised Steve I'd water his plants today" I said.
"He has a house?" she asked
"Of course"
I thought he lived at the caff" she laughed.
"What's even more amazing is that he has plants" I said "Wait till you see it"
"I'm intrigued!"
We walked up to his place, and Chrissy said "This is

his house?" Incredulous.

"Erm, yeah. Why?" I was puzzled

"I mean, look at it. It's a picture postcard village thatched cottage"

"Yes.....?"

"Sorry. I just can't picture him in a house like this" she said laughing

"He bought it with Jasmine" I said coldly

"Oh shit. Sorry" she said awkwardly "I'm sorry. I feel awful"

"I'm kidding" I said "He sold their house. This was his parents' house."

"You fucker!" she shouted at me laughing and punched me on the shoulder. Again.

"Whoa! Language!" I said, laughing with her.

"Come on, let's go in"

She crept in behind me, clearly intrigued as to what the inside would look like.

"Oh my God" she said walking into the living room "This is NOT how I pictured the inside"

"You think he lived in some sort of flashy bachelor pad?" I asked

"Yes! Exactly. This is beautiful" she said looking around "And these photographs, stunning"

"All him" I said

"Fuck off" she said incredulously.

"Wow, you need to watch your mouth young lady" I said. "Yes, all him. He's a great photographer. He loves the outdoors"

"Wow. Goes to show you never *really* know someone" she walked around looking at the framed landscapes from Steve's travels. "These are really good" she said, still amazed.

"Not just a foul-mouthed Casanova" I said

"No, it appears not" she said. "And look at the decor, it's so......."

"Nice? Traditional?"

"Yeah. He's got great taste. And there are so many plants"

"Speaking of which, I have a job to do" I said, and disappeared into the kitchen.

Chrissy was still wondering around with her mouth agape, clearly impressed.

"Yeah, of course" she said absent mindedly.

I went around and watered all the plants, each one as per its own strict instructions hammered into me by Steve.

When I'd finished, I found Chrissy in the dining room, staring at a small frame. I knew it well.

"That's Jasmine" I said. I obviously startled her.

"Jesus! Sorry, I didn't mean to nose" She put the picture down.

"It's ok" I assured her "She's a big part of him"

"She was VERY pretty" she said

"Yeah, she was lovely, and his entire world. Such a shame"

"Poor Steve. It must be hard for him" she said

"Yeah, it was tough for a long time"

She punched me on the shoulder again, hard.

"Ouch! What the...?"

"I don't want to be the one left with only a picture of you. So, you promise me right now that you'll

never try that again"
"What?" Another punch.
"You heard. Promise" Holy crap, she was pretty angry.
"Jesus, I promise" Rubbing my sore shoulder.
"You saw the effect it had on Steve. I don't want to be that person. Don't you dare do that to me"
"Ok, ok." I said. She had made her point. And made it well. "I promise"
"On your kids' lives?"
"On my kids' lives. I promise I will never try that again"
"Good. Now take me home. I'm hungry."
I locked the door, and we walked back to her aunt's house.
"Where we going?" she asked
"You said take me home..." I began.
She cut me off "To yours, you muppet."
"Ah" I said, and we kept walking
"You know you're beautiful when you're angry" I said
The expected shoulder punch came hard and fast
"Ouch! What??"
"Don't be a dick Jack" she said annoyed.
"Sorry" I said.
"But thank you" she winked.
We held hands for the rest of the way.

My God, I loved this woman. I would never do anything to hurt her.

I know what you're thinking; why has Steve got

a picture of Jasmine in his house when he's with Willow now? Or even if you weren't, I think it's worthy of explaining. Imagine yourself in his shoes. What would you do? Erase all traces of her? Or keep one small reminder of a better time? To keep her memory alive. Would Willow mind? I can't answer that question. But, I will tell you that the next time we were at his house; the picture was gone. Willow is an understanding and supportive type, who knows what she thought? All I know is that the memory of Jasmine lives on; a year later, they had a little girl, and they named her Heather Jasmine Fletcher. (Yes, Stephen Fletcher)

We got back to mine, and I made us a late lunch of fried egg sandwiches. Everyone loves a fried egg sandwich, and Chrissy was/is no exception. Whilst I was doing that, she was nosing around the garden. She came back in with a damning verdict; it was a mess. "Have you been talking to my mother?" I asked.
"No. Why??
"Nothing. You a gardener?"
"No, I lived in a flat remember. But, I love pottering around in my aunt's garden. I could make this work" She said confidently.
"Well, feel free" I said "I'm not a gardener, that was her thing."
"Leave it to me. It'll be a bee paradise before you know it"
"A bee paradise?" I asked

"It's important to provide food for bees Jack, they're in decline, and we need them"
Oh shit. I thought, please not an environmentalist.
"Don't get me wrong" she took a sip of tea and continued "I'm no eco warrior, but I care about bees"
Pfew. "Well, like I said, you do whatever you want. The garden is not my territory"

I should add here that I had an ulterior motive here; I really wanted the garden changing; Helen had made it her own place, and it just reminded me of her. Hence I'd let it go completely. Chrissy would go on to make it beautiful, completely different to Helen's tastes. Thankfully.

"Where are the kids?" I thought out loud.
"Maybe your parents took Elsie for lunch. What time did James say he'd be home?"
"Around lunch."
"Have you checked your phone recently grandad?" she mocked.
"Funny." No, I hadn't in fact. I pulled my phone out and checked for messages; 2 from James saying he'd be home around 3 (he was playing football with his mates). And mum; they had indeed taken Elsie for something to eat over in Ramsey. They'd be back around 2 ish. I checked the time; 13.48.
"Elsie will be back soon, they've gone to Ramsey for lunch, James around 3"
"Told you" she nudged my elbow.
"Hmmmm" I said.

We sat in silence for a bit; me checking my emails, and Chrissy no doubt buying the world's supply of flowering plants. 20 mins or so later, Elsie ran into the kitchen. They'd had a fantastic afternoon, and she's had a pink glazed doughnut after her lunch. Mum and dad seemed revitalised; Elsie had that effect on them. She was so full of life. Don't get me wrong, they took James out too, but he was older that Elsie, and had lost a lot of his childishness. If that makes sense. He was more grown up. They were different characters. Elsie boisterous and full of life, James more reserved and teenager like. It was an age thing. I think my parents were taking all the opportunities they could with Elsie before she too became a morose teenage zombie.

Mum suggested that they took the kids back to theirs for dinner, and that they could sleepover if I wanted? I asked the kids. Unanimous; yes. "There, now you don't have to worry about hurrying home tonight" mum said to me with a knowing look. Not sure what she was thinking, but she was wrong on this count. We were going out for food and a few drinks. There would be no funny business. Not that she had any way of knowing that of course.
They had a quick cup of tea, then rounded the terrible twosome up and they were gone.
Just like that. The storm had given way to silence.

Minor tangent.

The storm had given way to silence. What does

that intimate? Here's what I meant; the whirl of social interaction was gone. That's how a socially anxious person thinks. We can only stomach a certain amount of social interaction. Hence you don't see Jack out all the time, or spending hours chatting to Steve at the café. Short, sharp interactions, then the headphones go on to drown out the noise of social interaction around him. And that doesn't mean he doesn't love his kids and parents. It just means he needs "Me time".

I was tired. The last few days had been draining. I was happy, and positive, but just tired. This would be the story for the rest of my life; always tired. Mental tiredness. It's tough.

Don't know how, but Chrissy could tell. "Hey, I'm going to pop back and see my aunt for a bit. Why don't you go up and get your head down for a few hours?"

"You sure?" I asked.

"You look tired" she stroked my cheek "Go get some rest"

"You're right. I'm exhausted"

"One favour though? Take a pill now please?"

I popped a pill from the strip and swallowed it with the last of my tea. "All done nurse" I said.

"How did you know I have a nurse outfit?" she asked curiously.

"Wha...?"

"I'm kidding. Go get some sleep my love. I'll be back at 5. I'll take a key just in case" She kissed me and left. Yeah, I love her. Who wouldn't?

I tidied away the cups, and went upstairs. Headphones in, I managed about 5 minutes of Victorian London before I was comatose.

I woke to a soft kiss on my cheek. I took a moment with my eyes closed to enjoy the closeness, the smell. Then I opened up and re-joined the world.
"Hey sleepyhead" She was beautiful. My god.
"Here, I made you a coffee" she handed me a steaming mug as I sat up.
"What time is it?" I asked, still a bit drowsy.
"It's almost half five"
"Shit. You been here long?" I asked, taking a sip of coffee "Why didn't you wake me?"
"You looked so peaceful. I've just been sat here watching you sleep for a bit"
"Weirdo" I said, drinking more coffee
"Maybe, but I'm your weirdo" she said and kissed me on the cheek. "Now get up and have a shower, we should get ready"
I did as I was told, and had a nice long shower. So long in fact that Chrissy was banging on the door telling me to get out.
I dressed, and found her downstairs, opening a beer. "Finally! Talk about leisure showers!" she said.
I looked at her, but couldn't speak.
"You ok?" she asked, voice tinged with concern.
"I, erm"

"What's up? You ok?"
"You look stunning." I blurted out.
"What?" mixture of anger and embarrassment. She blushed.
"You look stunning" I re-affirmed. "Like, wow"
"Sod off you idiot" she said coyly. "I thought something was wrong"
"Something is wrong" I said "All eyes are going to be on you tonight. I'm going to have to be on my guard all night"
"You're a dick" she said laughing.
"I'm a very lucky dick" I added.

We went off for our big night out. The George wasn't quiet, being a Saturday night and it being the only pub around. But, we eventually got a table, and had a great meal. Conversation was good, if not a bit strained because of the noise levels. We had good chats about the holiday, the garden, Steve and Willow, the kids, and each other. It was a great evening. We danced a bit, and I introduced her to some of the locals (the ones I knew). She was a hit. And why wouldn't she be? This gorgeous, confident, smiley vision of perfection. Wow.

Last orders kind of was our reminder to leave. I had to be semi-fresh for the kids tomorrow.

I walked Chrissy back to her house. It was late, and it was cold. We stood awkwardly at the front door for a bit, like a pair of shy teenagers. It was the drink, and we both knew it. Eventually, I kissed her and said goodnight. It was weird, we both wanted more, but knew we should wait.

I walked home in a daze. I guess mostly due to the booze, but also just madly in love. Tonight has proven we were good together; we were able to talk, non-stop, all night. About the most random things at times, but there were no awkward silences. It was all good. I was happy. Again, likely due to the 7 pints we'd knocked back over the course of the evening. We had bonded well over the last few days; she had seen me at my lowest and highest, and hadn't ran away. Over the years to come, she would see me at my lowest on several occasions, but she's still here.

I got home, and plonked down on the bed. I just about had the state of mind to get changed, then crawled under the duvet.

Sleep came instantly.

DAY 7

Sunday, 23rd of March.

Oh my god. My head hurts. I woke with a dry mouth, and a banging headache. I needed water, urgently. I crawled out of bed and went down to get myself a pint of water. I downed it in one and crawled back up to bed. Sleep.

Don't know what time that was, but I woke a while later to see it was 06.34. My head wasn't banging quite so badly, but I still felt like shit. I go up and had a long shower to try wake my body. It worked. To a degree. Slowly got dressed and went to find something to eat. Scrambled eggs. Made all the difference. I felt better by miles after. I picked up my phone and had a look. Wasn't expecting much, but there were several messages from Chrissy. All sent early this morning. What? Seemed totally out of character. I opened them up, and almost dropped my phone.

01.44: Jack, at hospital with Mary, she had a heart attack. Call me.

01.58: jack, please call me

02.32: please jack

Fuck.

I dialled her number immediately, but no answer. Within seconds, my phone rang.
"Hey, what's happening, everything ok?" I asked
Crying on the other end. Shit
"She's gone Jack"
Fuck.
Shit.
She'd needed me, and I'd let her down.
"Oh my god Chrissy, I'm so sorry" I said. "I'm sorry, I was asleep"
"It's ok Jack, there's not much you could have done"
Wrong. I could have been there for you. I was angry. At myself.
"Are you still at the hospital?" I asked
"Yes. Will you come?"
"I'll be there in 20 minutes"
I called off, got dressed, and jumped in the car. Took about 15 minutes to get to the hospital, and almost as long to find somewhere to park. Fucking hell.
I ran inside but didn't have a clue where she would be. I didn't need to; there she as. Sat in the cafe, crying into a cup of coffee. I hurried over and held her n my arms.
"I'm so sorry my love, I'm so sorry. What happened?"

"She had a massive heart attack in ICU, they couldn't save her."

Fucknation. I wasn't good with this kind of thing. I thought furiously of things to say.

In the end, she didn't really need me to say anything; just to be there.

Her aunt had passed away just after arriving at the hospital, and Chrissy had been sat here, alone for over 4 hours. I felt like the worst person in the world.

"I'm sorry I wasn't here for you" I offered

"It's ok Jack, not your fault, you were asleep." she said

"Let me take you home. There's nothing more you can do here" I said

"I can't leave her Jack" she said with a hint of confusion.

"Hey, it's your turn to listen to me now. Let me take you home. There isn't anything you can do for her"

I got her back to the car, and we drove home in silence. When we got there, I took her straight upstairs and put her in my bed. She started to protest, but I cut her off "You need to sleep"

No further argument, she lay down, and drifted off to sleep. I sat watching her for a while, thinking about how I had let her down. She had been there for me, and the one time when she needed me, I had failed her. I went down and took my pill, as I could feel myself heading in the wrong direction. This was not going to be about me. It couldn't be. I needed to be able to focus on my love. I made myself a coffee, grabbed a laptop from the office, and set up camp on the bed, next to her. I would at least be there for her when she woke up.

She stirred at around 9, and I went down to get her a bottle of water. I put it on the bedside table, ready for when she woke. At about 10.30, she woke up, and hugged into me. "Thank you" she said. "I did nothing" I said guiltily. "I should have been there for you earlier."

"Not your fault Jack, don't beat yourself up over it" I wasn't going to; t*his was about her remember??*

"I still can't believe it" she said "She had some chest pain so woke me up. I recognised the signs, so called an ambulance. She seemed ok when they got there, just a bit of pain in her arm."

"You did what you could" I said

"I know, but she seemed ok. Next thing I know, they came out and told me how sorry they were, but she had suffered another heart attack, and they were unable to save her" She started crying as she spoke.

"Shhhh, it's ok." I comforted her as best I could, given my limited abilities.

"I need to call people to let them know" she said suddenly.

"Right now?"

"I need to let my cousins know their mother died Jack"

"Are you up to it?" I asked, "I could do it for you if you want?" I knew she'd say no, but I had to ask.

"No, it's ok, I'll call them" she picked up her phone. "I'll give you some privacy" I said and went downstairs and left her to make the dreaded calls.

15 Minutes later, she came down and sat at the kitchen table. "That was the hardest thing I've ever had to do" she said and started crying again.

"You did good, I'm sure they think the same" I kissed the top of her head, and just held her for a bit.

"Would you like me to get you something to eat?" I asked "I can do some scrambled egg if you want it"

"That would be great, if you don't mind. Could I ask for a coffee and some headache tablets too please?"

"Of course, you can" I went off and made her a coffee and gave her two paracetamol's with it.

She downed the tabs with a few sips of coffee and sat with her head in her hands. "What am I going to do Jack?" she said. "Her kids are in New Zealand. Should I look into trying to organise stuff? I don't know"

"Are they coming over?" I asked

"They'll be here by Wednesday" she said.

"There isn't an awful lot for you to do in the meantime" I suggested. "They will need to speak to the hospital and organise everything as they are the next of kin"

"You're right, but I just feel like I should be doing something for her" she sounded helpless

"Hey, there's nothing for you to do." I said "I'll call mum and ask her to keep the kids there. You can crash here for a while if you like. Who's looking after the dog?"

"No, I don't want to be sat in misery, having the kids around would help." she paused "Does that sound weird?"

"Not at all. I always feel miles better whenever they are around" I said "Makes perfect sense"

"Thanks. And the neighbour has the dog, she loves him so doesn't mind. I would like to get changed though, do you have anything I could borrow? I really don't want to go back to the house right now

"I'm sure I could throw something together" I said "As long as you don't mind wearing my boxers"

That resulted in yet another punch to the shoulder, but a smile went with it. Result.

I went off and sorted her out with some clothes whilst she went to have a shower.

When I called mum and told her the news, she was terribly upset; she had known Mary since they were children. I asked her not to tell the kids. She wanted to know if I wanted to keep them here and bring them back after dinner. I said Chrissy wanted to have the kids around to take her mind of things, but then had an idea. Mum was doing a roast today, and I think a cosy family roast would be just what she needed. Plus, she could talk to my mum, who was infinitely better at consoling people than I was. I told mum we'd be there in an hour or so.

Once she had sorted herself out and gotten

dressed, I asked Chrissy if that is something she'd want to do. She hugged me and said it's exactly what she needed right now.

When we got there, mum gave her a massive hug and took her off into the kitchen. I went to see the dynamic duo, who were giving dad a hard time on the PlayStation. "Not really my thing" he said looking at me pleadingly.

"Hey gang, why don't we give grandad a rest eh" Thankful looks from dad.

"Ok dad, you want to play?" James asked.

"Erm, no, you guys carry on. I said.

"How's things going son?" dad asked as we walked into the dining room, "Is she ok?"

"She's better than she was" I said. "She was pretty bad when I picked her up from the hospital"

"Poor thing, she must be terribly upset"

"Yeah. Doesn't help that Mary's kids live in New Zealand" I said

"They're good kids" he said "I'm sure they'll be here in a flash"

"They're getting here Wednesday" I told him

"Ah, yes, good kids see"

I hoped so. Chrissy wasn't able to make any of the arrangements or sign anything as she wasn't the next of kin. I was hoping Mary's kids would come over and sort everything out. And, turned out they did. They are/were good as gold.

We had our roast dinner, and it was a great family occasion. Chrissy fitted in perfectly, she was in on all of the conversations, and having a good old laugh at some of mum's stories. It was perfect. She was keeping a brave face and making the most of the opportunity to forget. I was so proud of her.

As it got closer to going home time, I pulled her aside in the kitchen. This was going to be awkward.
"Hey, I was kind of wondering what you were doing tonight? I mean, are you staying at home? You're more than welcome to stay at mine." I quickly added "As in, I have 2 spare rooms."
"Would you mind?" she said
"Of course not. You know that. Would you like me to ask mum to go and get you some stuff from your place?"
"You think she would?"
"Duh. Of course. Just let her know what you want, and I'll take her over"
She went off to talk to mum, and the two of us went over with a list and the keys.
I waited outside, whilst mum went in and got all the stuff on Chrissy's list. She eventually came out with a bag. "Think I got everything. Got a few days' worth of clothes. Just in case"
"Thanks mum" I said.
"Poor girl must be devastated. You make sure you take care of her" She said
"Yes mum"
We drove back and went re-joined the family inside. I rounded up the kids, and we got ready to

go. Mum and dad fussed over the kids as we said our goodbyes, then drove over to Ramsey to drop the kids at my ex in-laws.

Once we were done, we drove back in silence. I sensed that this was possibly not the time for humour or conversation of any sort. Sometimes it's just better to say nothing.

Back home, I left Chrissy on the sofa and went up to make up Elsie's bed for her. It was a double, and I thought she'd be more at home in a girl's room. Once done, I joined her on the sofa.

"How are you doing?" I asked.

"I'm ok" she reassured me "Can we just watch tv and cuddle up?"

"Yeah sure" I said "Anything in particular you want to watch?"

"I don't mind, I just need to lie here with you" she replied and cuddled up to me.

I selected an episode of Sherlock, and we lay there watching until I noticed she'd fallen asleep on me. "Hey, come on, let's get you to bed" I said. It was only just after eight, but she had had an emotionally draining day.

I took her upstairs and got her settled in Elsie's room, then said goodnight and went back downstairs to give her some privacy to get ready and go to bed.

After another beer, and finishing the episode, I went to bed myself.

Did my usual of going over the events of the day whilst lying in bed.

It had been a hell of a day, and I hoped the following days would get better. Even if only slightly.
I put my headphones in and hailed a Hansom to take me to 221b Baker Street.
Sleep didn't come easy but did eventually.

I woke around 3am to find Chrissy had joined me and was asleep cuddled up to me. I held her, and eventually drifted back to sleep. Yeah, no funny business in this book.

I was taking care of the woman I loved, she needed this, and I wasn't going to let her down.

DAY 8

Monday, 24th of March.

I opened my eyes and saw on the alarm clock that it was 07.12. Chrissy was still asleep in my arms. I let go ever so gently and managed to get out of the bed without waking her. I went downstairs and made her a cup of tea. I didn't really know if she drank tea in the morning, but thought it was the right thing to do.

When I got back upstairs, she was sat up in bed, scrolling through her phone.

"Morning" I said putting the tea on the bedside table.

"Morning. Thanks for letting me stay" she said. "I really needed company"

"No problem" I said with a smile. "Glad to be able to do something for you"

"I have so much work to do this week, not sure if I can face it" she confessed.

"Work always helps keep my mind from drifting the wrong way" I offered "It would be good to take your mind off things"

"You're right, thanks" she said, sipping her tea.

"I wasn't sure if you drank tea in the morning" I said "I just thought it was the thing to do"
"Well, usually, I don't. But today, it's exactly what I needed" she smiled "Thanks"
"Speaking of work," I said "Did you want to work from here, or do you need to go back?"
"I need to go back" she said, a bit down. "But I need to go back at some point right?"
She was right. Hiding away from it all was the wrong thing to do. I had an idea.
"Hey, erm, I can work from anywhere, as long as I take my laptops. You want me to come with and work from there today?"
"Would you mind?" she asked, the relief obvious
"Of course not. I'll go pack up my stuff while you have a shower and get ready"
She leaned over and kissed me "Thanks" she said "For everything"
I kissed her back and went off to my office to pack up what I needed.

We walked over to the house, and stood outside for a long moment, neither of us speaking.
I broke the silence "Hey, we don't have to do this if you're not ready"
"No, I want to. I'm just… you know"
"It's ok. Take your time."
We stood for a minute or so longer, before she took a deep breath and opened the door. We walked in, and stood for a moment, taking it in. The place was obviously exactly as her aunt had left it, and

I followed Chrissy's gaze; her empty teacup still on the coffee table, a magazine on the arm of her chair, her reading glasses on top of it, shopping list half written on a small note pad on the dining table. Purse right next to it. It was all too much. She started crying.

"Hey, we don't have to stay here if you don't want to."

"I'm sorry" she said, "I thought I could"

"It's fine. Let's just grab what you need and head back to mine"

"Right, give me a few minutes" she disappeared upstairs, and gathered what work items she needed, and some fresh clothes in a bag.

"Ok, I have everything I need" she said solemnly "There shouldn't be any need for me to return before my cousins get here."

"Sure?" I asked

She looked through the bag, and confirmed "Yes, I have everything. Can you take me home please?"

"Of course, come on"

We left the house, and didn't return until almost a week later.

We got back, and I told her she was free to use my office as her own; I could easily set up camp on the kitchen table. She protested against evicting me from my own space, but I insisted.

"It's ok, I can work from anywhere; you make yourself comfortable."

She hugged me "Thank you" a kiss, "For everything"

"I'm just trying to make sure you're happy" I said. "Give me a moment, and I'll clear you a drawer and some wardrobe space in Elsie's room.

"You don't have to…" but I cut her off "Yes, I do. Can't have you living out of a bag"

"Fine. At least let me make you a coffee" she said

"That would be marvellous" I smiled.

I'd emptied two drawers, and half the wardrobe for her. I put Elsie's stuff in my wardrobe for the time being. *Is that enough. Are you sure you're doing enough? Trying hard enough?* Yes I am dammit, leave me alone. I shrugged it off and went back downstairs.

"Top two drawers, and half a wardrobe, plenty of hangers. Is that going to be enough, or do you need more?"

"Jack, it's perfect, thank you. Here, sit down" she motioned at the mug on the table. I sat opposite her. My phone buzzed. I checked it, and found a message from Steve

Him: Hey dickhead, back in town! You fancy a pint later?
Me: Welcome back matey! Let me talk to Chrissy, it's been a bit of a tough weekend for her
Him: Oh yeah…. Wink wink. You stud
Me; No, you knob, her aunt died.
Him Oh fuck, sorry mate. She ok?
Me: She's up and down. I'll have a chat with her and let you know
Him: Ok mate

Me: Hey
Him: What?
Me: Good to have you back
Him: middle finger emoji

I smiled to myself. "Something good?" Chrissy asked
"Steve. They got back today. He wants to know if we want to meet up for a drink later"
"That would be good, I'd love to hear about the holiday" she said brightly
"It's a date then" I smiled. "Seven?" She nodded.
I text Steve back to let him know we'd meet them at 7 in the George.
2right, now, time to get to work" I said
"Mmm, yes, I'll leave you to it." she said, finishing her coffee. She got up, kissed me, and disappeared off upstairs.
I flashed up my laptops, and checked emails; quite a few videos this week, but short ones. Should have this done by Thursday. Result. I got to work.

We both paused for lunch just after twelve, and had a sandwich and a chat about the holiday. It was all very positive; working was doing her good. Likewise, I was feeling very positive myself today. Work had a bit to do with it, but Steve being back home was what really did it. It was good to have my buddy close. Plus, the cafe would be open again. All good.
I finished up around 15.30, and had a look in the fridge & cupboards. Shit. I needed shopping.

I could hear Chrissy upstairs, she was talking to someone; probably an online meeting. I picked up my phone and sent her a text.

Me: Hey, didn't want to disturb you. I need to go out to the shop. Won't be long

Her: Thanks, just in the middle of a meeting

Me: You need anything?

Her: Not really, I'm good ta

Me: Ok, see you in a bit. X

Her: X.

I grabbed the keys and drove over to the supermarket in Ramsey.

The shop in Ramsey was not massive, just a Co-op local, but it had a wider range of stuff than our local shop. We walked around, and quickly filled the small basket I was carrying. Chrissy was going to make dinner, and it involved steak. I love steak. I love this woman.

On the drive home, she asked if we could have a chat. Something had been on her mind, and she wanted to talk about it. Fuck. What? *It's you, it's definitely you.* Shut up! We got home, put the shopping away, and I made us a cup of tea.

"What's on your mind?" I asked, tentatively.

"Oh, hey, it's nothing to worry about" she said "I've just been thinking about something"

Vague. She's usually really forthright with things, extreme confidence and all that. What's going on? *It's totally you. She's had enough of cry baby Jack.* Shut up dammit.

"I'm listening" I said, taking a sip of tea to hide my anxiety, but probably failing.
"How do I put this?" she thought for a second. That second was long enough for my inner voice to give me a good kicking…
"I want to talk about sex Jack"
I almost spat my tea out. She laughed. "Relax stud, not right now"
"Yeah, I wasn't thinking that" not convincing… "What about it?"
"I feel like it's something we haven't talked about, or approached. It's quite a natural thing, and I just don't want you to get the wrong idea"
I looked quizzical "About…"
"About me not taking things further?" she answered, with an expectant look.
"I haven't thought about it to be honest" I said. And I was lying. I had. A lot. *Pervert!* Sod off.
"I know you're lying!" she laughed "Look at me, how could you possibly resist?" she added, still laughing.
Yes, I am looking at you. I thought. And I want to tear your clothes off, but it just doesn't feel right. *Tell her that you wimp!* What? Oh yeah…
"You're right" this was difficult! "I'm not really sure. That is, I am. But…" trying to think of the right words…
"But? You don't want to?" Shit. This was going in the wrong direction!!! Abort! Abort! Sort it out Jack!!! Now!
"No! No, I erm. Oh shit, this is going to sound

weird"

"Try me" staring intensely. Fuck.

"I doesn't feel like the right time?" I said, worried.

She sighed with the greatest relief. "That's exactly what I was thinking." she said. I could see the weight disappearing off her shoulders. She visibly relaxed.

"It was?" I asked, equally relieved.

"Yes. I fancy the pants off you Jack, I really do. But I also think you're not in the right place right now, and neither am I. It would be better to wait until we're both in a good place"

"I couldn't agree more" I said "Don't for a second think that I don't want to. I do, a lot. Like, a lot, a lot." She giggled. "And you are right, my head is all over the place, and it just feels wrong at the moment. I'd rather wait until the time when it'll be perfect"

"That's very sweet Jack. Thank you" she leaned over and kissed me. "I knew you'd understand, and to be fair, I haven't been sat here worrying why you hadn't jumped on me yet. I know you have your issues. And I have my own to deal with." What issues? Decided not to push it, she would tell me in her own time.

"Perfect. Can we talk about something else now?" I asked, "Something less awkward?"

"Like what?" she laughed.

"Like steak. I'm hungry. Get on with it. I'll supply drink while you cook"

"Deal" she laughed.

We go to it. (Not that!) Talking holiday plans, and a fair warning that boxes of plants were going to turn up on Friday. "You're nothing if not predictable Miss Lenoir" I said. Cue shoulder punch. Ouch!

The steak was beautiful. Well cooked, and the company was charming. I told her as much, and she blushed. Sore another for the Jack! I thought. It's funny how compliments melt the confidence façade.

You have time for a tangent? Tough.

Sex. The chat about sex was uncomfortable. Don't get me wrong, I'm not shy in that respect. It was more because of the underlying issues. My head, my head, and... my head. *Hey! What about me??* Fuck you inner voice, this doesn't concern you.
Sounds really woolly; it's not the right time. But it really wasn't. *Worried about performance anxiety Jackie boy?* Will you fucking do one!? This does not concern you. Ok, in a way I was. *Ha! See? You'll be a flop! Get it? See what I did there?* Last time; fuck off! There was that a little bit, but also, it honestly wasn't really on my mind. Well, not a lot anyway. Did I want to? You bet! It just didn't feel right. Does that make sense? And it had nothing to do with Helen; she was historic data. I just felt very, very, fragile. And I desperately wanted to be a better man for her. I didn't want to fail her. I was sick of crying. I was sick of being anxious. I was sick of

it all. I felt like I was in the trough of the deepest wave ever, but was slowly starting to swim up. I needed to be at, or near, the crest of the wave. Then I would happily tear her clothes off. Anywhere, anytime. But for now, I was just happy that she'd addressed the elephant in the room. It was a great relief to have that conversation out of the way. I'm sure she felt the same. Right?

Back to the story… (Disclaimer: language going to get more colourful from here on…)

"Keep it up Mr Beckett. Scoring points will get you everywhere!" wink. *Keep it up! LOL! She'd be lucky! Jesus, will you fucking do one already???*
"Tease." I said "But I meant it. That was great."
"I'll take the compliment" she smiled
"Please do. Now, you stay here" I said, topping up her wine glass "and I'll sort the dishes"
"No argument there" she said with a smile.
I did the dishes, and tidied the kitchen. She was busy on her phone, hopefully not buying more plants…
"Right, done. It's five past six. You want to shower and get ready?"
"Mmm, good idea" she said, finishing her wine.
"You go first, Ill quickly check my emails"
She disappeared upstairs to have a shower, and I took my wineglass to the living room and flashed up the laptop. Couple of emails; all positive. No changes required. Good news.
"I'm done!" came the shout from upstairs. I shut

down and had a shower.

By the time I'd showered and dressed, she was thankfully waiting downstairs. I say thankfully; no hours spent doing make-up and hair. Minimal make-up, quick hair dry & ponytail. Perfection.

"Ready?" she asked, clearly proud that she was done before me.

"Yes ma'am." I said

We walked over to the George, my excitement growing as we got closer. "You ok?" she asked

"Yeah, just happy to have my friend back again" I confessed.

"You two are funny" she said smiling. We went inside.

Loud whistle. "Yo! Over here!" Steve standing by a table in the corner, beckoning us over "Got a round in you tightwad!"

We both laughed "It's good to have him back"

"Mate!" he said, arms open

We hugged. "Good to see you buddy" I said

"And you nutjob. How you been?"

"So-so mate, so-so. But surviving"

We swapped partners, and I asked Willow "How was he?"

"He was great" she winked. Oh, not what I meant, but message received.

We sat, and Steve made a toast "To the 4 amigos, may they always be together"

"Cheers to that" I said.

Chrissy went straight in "Tell us about the holiday! How was it????"

"It was great!" Willow said with the imaginable excitement. "The place, the weather, the people, the food…Oh, the food"

"The pizzas were top notch" Steve joked

"Ignore him" Willow laughed, punching him on the shoulder I exchanged a quick look with Chrissy

"We only had pizza once. There's more to Italy than pizza Stephen"

"Stephen?" I said, looking at him wide eyed.

"Fuck you" he replied.

Willow got her phone out, and showed us all the pictures; it looked fantastic.

"Wow, looks like you guys has a fantastic time" I said

"We did, can't wait to go back" Willow said

"Going back?" I looked at Steve

"Already booked for the summer mate"

"Nice. Very nice. Must be good to have a choice" I said

"Don't mind him, he's just jealous" Chrissy said "He's taking me to Florence"

"Been told I am" I chimed in.

"Whatever. We're going to Greece with the kids, and then he's taking me for an "us" break"

"Good for you" Willow said to Chrissy

"Oh I see how it is" I said

We all laughed. This was great. I had missed my mate.

"More drinks?" I asked

Another round was needed. I motioned to Steve to

come with me.

"You need help with four fucking drinks?" he asked as we walked to the bar.

"No you idiot. I was trying to give Chrissy and Willow some time to talk about her aunt"

"Ah, get it. How's she been?"

I ordered the drinks, and replied "She's getting better mate. She can't be in the house though, so she's staying at my place"

"Oh yeah, well played mate" he nodded, smiling

"No you moron, nothing like that. She's in Elsie's room."

"What?" he looked confused.

"It's not always about sex you muppet."

"It's not?"

"No!" my turn to punch his shoulder.

"Ouch! I'm only kidding you fuckwit!"

"I know" I smiled.

"You're not ready, even I can understand that" he said, rubbing his shoulder.

"You can?" Cue punch to shoulder… "Ouch!"

"Good. Prick."

"You opening up tomorrow?" I asked, changing the subject.

"You missed your hidey place?" he asked

"Fuck you. I'm being serious"

"Yes, we are. Went to the wholesaler this afternoon, all ready to re-open."

"Good. I missed Willow's coffee" I said

"Dick"

"Takes one to know one" I mocked

"Fuck me, you sound like a ten year old" he laughed.
We collected the drinks and returned to our ladies.
"Ladies" Steve said putting drinks down "miss us?"
"Like a hole in the head" Willow joked
"Funny. You're funny" he mocked.
"Wish I was as funny as you think you are" she replied laughing.
He shook his head in mock-disgust. "See what I have to put up with mate?"

The rest of the evening was just great. We had a few more drinks, and a lot more laughs. It was exactly what Chrissy and I needed. We went home with smiles on our faces.

We got home and changed into pj's, and said goodnight.
"Goodnight Mr Beckett" she said
"Sleep softly my love" I replied
We kissed and went to our separate beds.

No headphones. I was slightly drunk, and full of happiness.
I fell asleep almost as soon as my head hit the pillow.

DAY 9

Tuesday, 25th of March.

I'd like to start the day with a quick couple of points:

1. Jack, you hardly ever mention the cat.

You're right, I don't. I'm not an experienced writer, and I struggle just keeping the 4 main characters in the story, never mind a cat. The cat is well, and well looked after. The kids love her. She basically lives in Elsie's room when she's here. And Chrissy? Yes, she likes her too. Sits on her lap whenever she can. Is that enough about the cat? Cool.

2. Jack, you hardly ever mention speaking to your kids.

Again, my writing skills are not so great that I can fit all that in. Rest assured, I text my kids several times a day, and speak to them most evenings. We have our own chat group.

I've read plenty of books where it doesn't go into the absolute minutia of someone's existence. Just imagine it if you need to. Or deal with it if you lack imagination.

Just on that quickly, if I may; I have great communications with my kids. Speaking in the current tense, 10 years after this story… We text all the time. We speak almost every day. Do I have the same levels of comms with everyone else? No. Did it work well in the preceding 10 years? Fuck no. I got into trouble a lot for not telling either Chrissy or Helen what I had arranged with the kids.

It's so easy to miss someone out. Heed my warning and watch it; include everyone! Saves a lot of arguments.

Happy? Let's go back…

My God. My head hurt, and I couldn't be arsed to get up. My bladder, on the other hand, had other ideas; *Get up you prick, I'm full.* Gotcha. Ugh, let's go. I crawled out of bed to relieve my painfully full bladder. It was just after half 7, so I got in the shower straight after. Shower wasn't quite working its magic. FFS Jack, come on. Turned down the hot water. Yep, that did it. Holy shit.

I got dressed, and headed downstairs to down a pint of water with some headache tabs.

"Morning sunshine"

"Jesus!" I half shouted "I shit myself"

"Fucking time you call this you gimp?" Steve asked "Can't handle it anymore eh old man!"

"Fuck you man, it's too early. How the fuck you get in anyway?" I asked, my head pounding.

"I let him in" Chrissy came in from the garden. "You ok? You look like crap"

"Doesn't he just" Steve added. I did. She, on the other hand, looked fantastic. *How the fuck....* I thought.

I turned to Steve "You better have brought me coffee you prat"

"Mate, I live to please you" he said, nodding towards the coffee cup on the counter.

"You fucking star" I said, and headed straight for the cup.

"Look at him, he's like a feckin addict" Steve said to Chrissy

"Poor baby is feeling fragile today Stephen" she said in a mocking tone

"Jesus. Seriously? Both of you?" I popped a couple of ibuprofen. "And you young lady." I said, motioning my coffee cup towards Chrissy. "You're supposed to be on my side"

"Bless. Why don't you down that and come have breakfast at the caff" Steve said. "Sausage and egg bap on me"

"First intelligent thing you've said all morning" I winked "Let's roll"

"I'm going to give it a miss boys, some of us have work to do"

"You sure? I can stay?" I said

"Nope, you go. I have a video call with the CPS in 20 minutes" That explained why she looked so sharp.
"Ok, if you're sure"
"Yep, go. Get out of here you bum!" She said, motioning for me to get out
"Ok, Ok, I know when I 'm not wanted" I said grabbing my coat.
"Right" Steve said "Come on fucknut, I'll sort you out" putting his arm around me and leading me out.

Tinkle. Oh yes, it's good to be back. I thought with a smile.
"Hey Jack! How's the head today?" Willow called from behind the coffee machine. The place was full, and it made me feel self-conscious.
"He's a bit fragile toady dear, be gentle" Steve said, rescuing me.
"Poor thing. Have a seat, I'll get you a drink." Willow said looking at me around the machine.
Where? I thought. It's rammed. My usual table will be... Ah. Reserved. Nodding head in appreciation at Steve. "Noice"
"Full service matey" he said with a wink. "Sit yourself down"
I sat in my seat, and looked around; the usual morning crowd was in, and Willow was working the coffee machine like a demon. Steve disappeared off into the kitchen to start cooking.
There was something comforting about being here. Not only because of the food and drink, but

also the familiarity of the faces and the fact that my safety net was mere feet away from me should I fall.

I felt at home here. I was made to feel at home here. It was my safe place. I could escape here if I needed, and could work from here if I needed. I didn't like doing that too often, as I always felt like I was taking up valuable space for customers. Steve, obviously, thought I was talking shite whenever I mentioned that. He's a good guy. His brusque, unrefined exterior hides a man with refined talents and interests. He was a hell of a catch for Willow. And she was for him to. They fitted. Like the last two jigsaw pieces in the puzzle of life. Ooh, poetic. Like it.

Willow brought my coffee over and kissed my cheek "Hope you feel better soon" then trotted off back to the counter.

I sipped my coffee whilst staring out the window. The snow was starting to melt, dream landscape slowly disappearing. Shame. Though, it had been nice while it lasted. Soon we'd be back to usual rain.

A plate was chucked on the table, and broke the spell. "There, get that down you" Steve said "And don't even think of asking for sauce you cheeky sod" He walked off, back to his place in the kitchen. No sauce? What? I took a bite. Oh. Good. Soooo good. And the bugger had already put brown sauce on it. Legend.

I savoured every mouthful of this heaven sent

food, I needed it so much. I let out a satisfied sigh when I'd finished, which solicited bemused looks from most of the ladies in the café. I took my plate and cup over to the counter. "Hey Willow, thank you for saving my life. That was superb. Please pass my thanks on to your kitchen maid"
She laughed "You're welcome sir"
I said goodbye and went home; work to be done.

Closed the door behind me and took off my coat. I could hear talking upstairs, indicating Chrissy was busy. I went into the kitchen and set up my office for the day, and got to work. Fortunately all short videos this week, so plenty of variety. I got stuck into some of the "Shorts" from my new client. Shorts were a new phenomenon, think tiktok style; short, attention grabbing videos. Deceptively hard to do; you have to get them just right, or people will not watch them. Managed 8 of these by around 1400. I took a break, and got myself a drink. Chrissy joined me about ten minutes later.
"Wow. What a meeting." she said, looking exhausted. "It was only supposed to be about an hour or so. Later almost 4. I'm pooped." She plonked herself in a chair. "You mind if I make a sandwich?"
"What's mine is yours, please don't ask; just help yourself"
"Thanks Jack" she got up and fixed herself a cheese sandwich "you want anything?"

"No thanks, I'm good" I said. I was still full from breakfast, and also still not feeling 100%.
"I'm so tired" she said, back at the table. "Early night for me tonight, sorry"
"Hey, don't be. I'll probably do the same"
She was sat scrolling through her phone, whilst eating. She looked beautiful, even when she must be feeling anything but.
"You got much left today?" I asked
"Not really, that meeting was basically it for the day. Not sure I could face much more anyway. How about you?"
"Well, I'm basically done for the day. If I start again, I'll be here till about 6 doing this, and I'm not feeling it to be honest. You fancy getting out for a walk?"
"Sure. Outside sounds great right now"
"How about up at Holme Fenn? It's still dry, so won't be muddy yet. We can walk around the lake"
"Deal. Let me finish up. I'll be down in ten." she disappeared back upstairs to finish up, and I did the same down here.

Hey loser, isn't that where you and Helen used to walk all the time? Feeling a bit nostalgic are we? Fuck off. It's a nice walk, and nothing to do with Helen, or you.

Grrr. Bloody inner voice. Holme Fenn is a nice nature reserve, about 3 miles up the road. There is a nice walk around the forest, and the lake. I liked it; it was quiet, and beautiful. I used to go running there a lot with Helen, but it didn't feel right anymore after she left. Enough time has passed not I think. I wasn't just going to avoid places because I used to go there with her. I'd have to stop going to almost anywhere if I started thinking like that.

We drove the short distance in silence. For a moment, I thought she had fallen asleep, but she was just staring out the window. Sometimes silence is indeed golden. Just leave it be.

The walk around the lake was awesome. There were swans, geese, ducks, and herons galore. There was a little small talk, nothing too heavy. Mostly about the kids, and if I wanted her to clear out for the weekend so I could spend time alone with them. I told her not to be silly; she was part of us now. Tough shit lady, you're stuck with us now. Ok, so in that case, what were we going to do with them this weekend? Did we want to go anywhere? I wasn't sure. I thought James said he had a football thing on Saturday. We could take Elsie somewhere though. "How about into the city? I know a cracking place to go for lunch"

"Sounds good, she'd like that. I might give you ladies a bit of space and go off on my own for a few hours. What do you think" I said. I obviously shocked her, or caught her unawares.

"You want to leave me alone with your kids?" she asked. How odd. I thought. Why would she ask that?

"Yes....why? You don't want to?" I asked, a bit confused

"Oh yes. I just didn't think you'd be ok with that yet." she seemed genuinely worried.

"Eh? Look here Christelle. You're part of my family now, and I think Elsie would love to spend some time with you."

"Christelle? Wow, it must be serious. Only my mum ever called me that"

"Don't be daft. I'm trying to be serious dumbass" I said

"Dumbass?" punch to shoulder...

"Ouch!"

"Serves you right. I was kidding you muppet" she laughed.

"Ah. I see. Well, in that case..." I started showing her towards the lake

"No! No! Jack! Stop it! No!" laughter filled with genuine fear. Funny.

"You're lucky you're so good looking! I said. "Wouldn't want to spoil those looks with dirty pond water"

"Ha ha. You're funny" she said, spun around, and pushed me into the water.

"What the...." I went down. Straight into the cold water. She thought it was fucking hilarious. I thought it was fucking uncalled for! However. What can you do? I laughed, and just said "Good one Lenoir. Well played" I held my hand out for her to help me up. She too it, and I pulled her in with me.

"Oh you dick!" she shouted "Oh1 Jesus! It's freezing Oh wow!" she scrambled up and got out. "You arsehole!" she shouted "I'm fucking freezing!" she was shaking. Both with fury and with cold. It was fucking hilarious. She was stuttering, and getting really annoyed because of it. "F f f f f fuck offfffff"

"Come on, let's get back to the car" I took her back to the car, both of us shivering with cold. Fortunately I kept a towel and some blankets in the boot. If you're a parent; you'll know why.

We dried off as best we could, and I wrapped her in two blankets to keep her warm. "W w what abbout y y y you?" She asked. It was hard keeping a straight face.

"Don't you worry about me" I said "It's only a short drive." I laughed Hard. The whole thing was farcical. Fortunately, she saw the funny side once a bit of warmth returned to her body, and she laughed too. Unfortunately, she tried to punch my shoulder, but couldn't quite manage it, resulting in more laughter from me, and a "F f f fuck y y y you" from her.

She jumped out of the car as soon as I parked up, and sprinted off towards the house "Fuck you Jack, I'm in the shower first!" Charming. She ran straight upstairs, leaving a trail of wet clothing for me to pick up. "Oh my God this feels soooo good!" she shouted from the shower. "Oh Jack, it's all hot and steamy". Giggles.

"Steady on Miss Lenoir, a lesser Gentleman would take advantage" I shouted back. Received with much giggling. "Oh Mr Darcy!" she just about managed between giggle fits. Just about.

What a woman. Damn. What a woman.
Did I mention that already? Tough shit.

I went down, and put the kettle on. I returned a few minutes later with hot cups of tea, just as she came out of the bathroom. "Ooh. Cheers me dear" she giggled, took a mug, and disappeared off into Elsie's room. "You're welcome!" I called after her. I drank some tea, then stripped off the wet clobber and had a shower myself. She was right; it was fucking great.
Totally refreshed, and feeling great, I got dressed. What a crazy afternoon. She was nuts. And people called me the nutjob!
I put the clothes in the washing machine, and called up to her
"Oi missus! You fancy a hot choc at the caff?"
"Yeah, be down in a sec" she yelled back
A few moment later, she came down, and I'll be damned if she didn't look fucking fantastic. Again. Hair in braids, dressed in the "athleisure" style, and just looking like perfection. I kissed her. Jesus, she smelled fantastic as well. Man… From drowned rat to a vision of beauty in 10 minutes. Jeez…
"You ok?" she asked
"Erm, yeah. Just looking" I said
"At moi?" she said and did a twirl. "You like the hair?"
"I like it all" I said before I could stop myself. "That is, I like the hair too"

She laughed. "My poor tongue tied boyfriend" she ruffled my hair.
I rolled my eyes "Yeah, whatever. Let's go".
"Lead on my good sir" she said, and we made our way over to the caff.

Tinkle

"Holy fuck! Don't you have a place of your own to live?" Steve said as we walked in
"Hello to you too" Chrissy said
"Not you my dear; that reprobate you just dragged in."
"Hey! Reprobates have feelings too you know" I protested
"What you want? It's almost closing time" he tapped his watch
"Hey guys" Willow smiled as she came in from the back. "Long time no see Jack"
"Oh look, another comedian" I said jokingly.
"Did I miss something?" she said, a bit unsure.
"Just him being a prize dick" I said
"Ah, nothing unusual there then" she nudged him in the ribs
"Hey! How did this become my fault?" he protested.
"Hmmm. Can I get you guys anything before I shut this down?"
"Hot chocs please, just plain. We need warming up" Chrissy said
"Why? What you been up to?" Steve asked.
We told him about our afternoon whilst we

savoured our hot drinks. Typical Steve response: "You bunch of fucking juvenile delinquents. How old are you? You'll do yourself an injury grandad"
"Hey!" Chrissy said. Punch to the shoulder.
"Ouch!" Steve rubbed his shoulder
"Don't insult the elderly" she added.
"Wow. Thanks dearest" I said, feigning hurt.
We all left together, after helping to tidy around.
"Things you do for a free drink eh!" I commented.
"Get out you prick." Steve said, pointing at the door.
And we did.

It was raining as we walked home, but we didn't care.
We got absolutely soaked, but we didn't care.
We were happy.

We got changed into pj's and lounged on the sofa, watching tv for the rest of the evening.
Everything was perfect.
Tomorrow might be different; the cousins arrive.

But for now, it was perfect. I held her in my arms until bedtime. It was pure bliss. Feeling her warmth, the sweet scent of whatever perfume she wears (I will find out), and the comfort of being with someone you love.

All too soon it was bed time. Damn.
I masked my disappointment, and we went our separate ways.
I lay in bed hoping tomorrow wouldn't be too bad

for her. Hopefully the cousins would be on top of things. Hopefully Chrissy would be able to deal with it without breaking down. Going backwards is not what she needed right now.

Headphones in, I walked into the foggy streets of Victorian London, where Holmes & Watson awaited...

DAY 10

Wednesday, 26th of March.

I woke, rolled my eyes in despair at how early it was. Dammit. Only 06.12. Why was I awake? Ugh. I got up, and the house was quiet. I looked out the window; not raining. Good, at least I could go for a run. Quietly, I changed, and went out for my run. I left Chrissy a note on the kitchen table, just in case. Waited for my GPS to go green, then started my run. It was very wet. The towpath was riddled with puddles, not a great day for running. Cold and wet are not my favourite combination of weather elements. I prefer cold and dry. I managed my standard 5k without getting too muddy, but my shoes were soaked through. I got home, dumped the shoes, and went for a shower.

After I'd dried off & dressed, I made myself a coffee, and scanned through my phone. Messages from the kids, mum, and... oh. Helen. What did she want? Please don't be bad, please don't be bad...

Her: Jack, the kids tell me they are going on holiday

this summer. Did you know Elsie needs a new passport? Let me know if you want to apply of if you want me to. I'll go half.

Ok, nothing bad. She was being nice. Why? No, don't fall in the trap; don't over-think it.

Me: You can do it if you like, you have all the required docs. Let me know how much I need to add and I'll transfer it.

10 secs later:

Her: Thanks, I'll do it later today.

Well, that wasn't bad I guess. I set up my office and got to work. About an hour later, I heard movement upstairs. I looked at my watch, it was almost half eight, seemed pretty late for her to be getting up. I shrugged it off and went back to work. The sound of her coming down the stairs made me look up. Here she comes, I thought, my vision of beauty. Oh. Erm, not today she wasn't. Still in her pj's, she looked pretty dishevelled. "Not working today?" I asked
"No, sorry, I should have told you. I don't really have anything today or tomorrow"
"Ah, alright for some" I said "Want a coffee?"
"No thank you, I'll just get a glass of water" she shuffled across to the cupboard, got a glass, and filled it. "You sure you're ok?" I asked
"Yeah, just tired. I'll be fine in a bit"
"Ok" I said, and decided to let it go. Don't push it,

she's probably anxious about today.

She finished her water and went back upstairs. Should I follow and see if she's ok? *No. Stay where you are, she'll come to you in her own time.* Yeah, good, ok. I'd finished 2 videos by 10.00, and had in the back of my mind that she still hadn't re-emerged. I got up, and went upstairs to find her.

I knocked on her bedroom door. No response. I quietly opened the door and peeked in; she was in bed, fast asleep. I gently closed the door and went back downstairs. This was unusual. Is this how she deals with anxiety? I guess people have different ways. Escaping into the land of dreams seemed as plausible as escaping to a coffee shop. If this was her way, then I should just let her be.

Shouldn't I? *Yes you should, and you're hungry too. And I fancy pastries.* Ok, you win.

I wrote her a note, grabbed my laptop, and made my way to my anxiety safe place.

No tinkle. Wait? Wtf? I thought as I walked in. "Where's the bell?" I called over to Steve.

"Broken mate, got a new one coming tomorrow, don't worry."

Cool. I chucked my stuff on my usual table, and went over to talk to my mate. "How's things today buddy?" I asked.

"Murder! No Willow today, she's off on a course" He looked tired.

"You penis. You should have called me, I would have come over to help" I said.

"Ach, it's done now." The man looked done-in.

"Dude, go sit, I'll get you a drink"

"Yeah, ok" he trudged over and sat down at my table.

I made us a cappuccino each, not brilliant, but they looked ok.

"Here" I said, putting it on the table. "You got anything left in the kitchen?" I asked

"Yeah, should be" he said, gratefully sipping his coffee

I went out back, and plated up some pastries for us.

"You're out of practice mate" I laughed "Here, eat"

"You're not fucking wrong mate, I'm beat."

"You look it. How long is she out for?"

"Should be back around 2 ish" he said

"Shit, you got to do lunch alone too?" I asked, alarmed

"Yeah"

"I'll stay"

"Mate, you have your own work" he protested.

"I'm ahead of schedule, I'll stay and help out"

"Life saver" he said, and we clinked cups.

"What course is she doing?"

"First aid. Apparently, I should have a first aider on site. Who knew?"

"That's a good this right? She can treat you when you keel over"

"Fuck you"

We sat for a bit, just chit chatting about stuff whilst finishing our coffees. When done, he went off to make sandwiches. "You need help?" I asked.

"Nah, you can man the coffee machine later mate if that's ok?"
"Absolutely."
I flashed up my laptop, and managed to finish another short video before the lunchtime rush.
The next couple of hours went by in a blur. No way he would have managed this on this own. No way. He knew it too; he gave me a massive hug when the surge had subsided. "Thanks man, I owe you one"

From behind me "Hi, can I get a coffee please?" I knew that voice
I turned. "Hey, you ok? I was worried" I leaned over the counter and kissed her.
"I'm good. Now. Just needed a good sleep. What you doing here?" she asked
"Willow is out, so I helped Steve with the lunch rush" I said
"Ah, cool. He's lucky to have you" she said with a smile
"Yeah, I am" Steve said from behind me
I rolled my eyes. "Go sit, I'll bring it over." She went and sat whilst I worked the machine and produced a nice latte. Wow, I thought. Once again she's gone from looking dishevelled to amazing. She was wearing jeans and a jumper, her hair tied back in a ponytail. Man…
"Thank you" she said, as I sat opposite her.
"Any news?" I asked tentatively.
"They've landed, and are on their way. Should get to Mary's about 3 ish"

I held her hands in mine "It'll be ok. You want me to come with you?"
"No, you don't have to do that, I'll be fine. Thank you though" she kissed me.
"Well the offer is there if you change your mind" I assured her.
We sat in silence for a moment. "You want to go for a walk or something before?" I asked
"You have time?"
"Yeah, I'm on track to finish tomorrow, so all good"
"Yes please then" she said gratefully.
I walked over to Steve to check if he was ok with me going "Mate, rush is over, you saved me. Go"
"Ok man, text me if you need me" I said
He chuckled. "That's my fucking line!"
"Laters mate" I said with a mock salute
I went back over to Chrissy, packed up my stuff, and we left Steve to it.

The weather wasn't brilliant, but it was dry. Still a chill in the air, but not as cold as last week. We walked across the bridge and down the tow path.

Little side note: I'd totally forgotten about the dog! I've just had to back and find an appropriate place to put in a few lines about it. Pfew! I only remembered because I had the following scene in my mind:

After a few minutes, we walked past a tree, and I laughed to myself. "What's up?" she asked
"Oh, just remembering how I got attacked by a

rabid dog and its lunatic owner over there not so long ago" I said

"Hey!" she punched my shoulder. Again.

"Ouch"

"He's a lovely dog, and I'm not a lunatic" she protested. "Not all of the time at least"

We hugged, and carried on. "What will happen to the dog?" she asked

"Don't know. I 'm guessing they can't take him to New Zealand" I said.

"Yeah, I kind of get that" she said mockingly. "I'm worried though…"

"Why?" I asked

"Well, I like him Jack, but not sure I have what it talks to be a dog owner. Going out in all weathers isn't my thing. Does that sound awful?"

"No, it doesn't" I reassured her "We're not all meant to be dog owners" I said.

"I feel bad though. What will happen to him?"

"Maybe the neighbour would want to keep him?" I suggested

"Dunno. I can ask I suppose. But, I'm not sure it's my place to do so. What do you think?"

"Why don't you wait till later on and discuss it with your family" I suggested

"Yeah, I will. He deserves a good home"

We got back to the house at just after half two.

"I want to go freshen up before I go" she said, and disappeared upstairs.

Five minutes later, she was back. I couldn't see any difference; she looked as amazing as before.

"You sure you don't want me to come? I asked her.
"No, it's ok. I should do this alone" she kissed me "You are amazing, thank you"
Not sure what I had done to deserve that comment, but I took it.
She put her coat on, and turned to me "I look ok?"
"You look amazing" I said.
We hugged, and she left. "Wish me luck" she said as she closed the door.
I stood for a moment in the hall, hoping it would all go well for her, and that she wouldn't come back broken.
Not much for me to do, I walked over and had a cup of tea with my parents to kill time. We talked for a while, and I told them about the dog. "We'd be happy to have him" she looked at dad for confirmation. He didn't disappoint "Of course. Good excuse to get out a bit more eh"
I thanked them, and said I'd mention it to Chrissy later.

When I got back home around six, Chrissy still wasn't back, so I decided to do a bit more work and get as far ahead as possible. There was also an email with a change request. I did that first and returned it to the client. I just about finished a video when my phone buzzed. She was on her way back. I finished up, and put my stuff away. I poured us both a glass of wine, and ordered in pizza.
I was there to greet her when she came in, and gave her a big hug "How'd it go?"

She took her coat off and followed me into the kitchen. She looked ok. Not upset, no signs of tears. She took a sip of wine and told me all about it.

Her cousins were really good about the whole thing. They'd appreciate her help in making all the necessary arrangement if that was ok. There wouldn't be a funeral; their mother had been against it. A direct cremation. There would be a private gathering to scatter her ashes at the lake in Holme Fenn. She always loved it there. I told her about my parents willing to take on the dog. "Wow, that's amazing. Are they sure?"

"Yeah, they'd love to. A good excuse to get out more"

"We had a chat about the dog, but we didn't really know what to do. I'll text them now to let them know" She picked up her phone and sent the message.

"I'm glad it went well. I was worried you'd be a mess when you got home" I said

"Bless, thank you. It was touch and go to be honest, but Jill and Pete were fantastic. They were so grateful that I'd been there for their mum. I t was really sweet"

"Good. I'm glad it turned out ok. That must be a huge relief" I said

"Yeah, it is. I haven't seen them for years. Apart from the circumstances, it was actually great to see them again"

"Brilliant" And I meant it. I was so happy for her. It could quite easily have been different. "What happens next?"

"Well, they're going to the hospital to see her and collect some paperwork so they can get a death certificate from the register office. Then, I think they're meeting with her solicitor to go through the will. If there's enough time."

"Wow, full day. Will you be joining them?" I asked

"Well, they've asked me too, and I said yes, but I wasn't happy to go to the solicitor with them. I said it's a family matter"

"What did they say?"

"Well, they said they were happy for me to come, but understood if I didn't want to." she said, a bit uneasy.

"Probably best to leave them to it" I said. And she agreed, obviously relieved.

"Yeah, I think so too" she seemed to drift off suddenly.

"Hey" I said, "come with me"

"What?" she asked confused

"Come, try something." I took her into the living room and turned on the hifi. "I want you to try something" I said. "You know Feeder?"

"Yes…"

"Right. I'm going to hit play, and we jump around like idiots for a few minutes. Guaranteed to energise you"

"You sure?" she looked sceptical.

"Just let go" I pressed play on the minidisc player, and Just a Day started blaring out.

She started hesitantly, but soon got into the

groove, and we jumped about like idiots for a few minutes, everything else forgotten about.
When the song ended, I asked her "Well?"
"You do this a lot?" she asked, panting
"Whenever I need to" I said smiling.
"It's fucking brilliant" she said "Such a release"
"Yep. It is. Never fails to get me in a good place."
"I can see why" she said laughing.
"Right, kick off your shoes, and let's go chill out with a movie."
"Fabulous idea" she said, and kissed me.
I fetched the wine bottle, and we sat on the sofa.
"What you wanna watch?" I asked
"Something funny please"
"Anchorman?" I suggested
"Not seen that" she admitted. I gave her a look.
"What? Are you kidding? It's a classic. How can you not have seen it? What's wrong with you?"
"Ok, ok, let's watch it" she said, punching me on the shoulder. Yet again.
The doorbell rang 10 minutes in.
"Who's that?" she asked
"Surprise" I said and went off to answer it.
I came back in and put a pizza box on her lap.
"Oh my God, I love you" she kissed me. Very nicely.
We ate pizza, drank wine, and watched the adventures of the Channel 4 News Team. She loved it. We both laughed like kids.

After the movie, I cleared up, and we went up to bed. Beds. She thanked me again, we hugger,

kissed, and went our separate ways.
I was on cloud nine. I'd just spent the perfect evening with the perfect woman. Could I possibly be this lucky? I decided that yes, I could be. I deserved to be.
I put my headphones in and called in at 221B Baker Street, but the narratives went unheard; I was in a fantasy world of my own. A perfect world where Chrissy and I were together. Where we were both happy. Where I was well. It was a great place, if not a few years away yet in reality.

I wasn't to know that.

For now it remained a fantasy.

I fell asleep happy.

Note: I feel I condensed quite a lot of stuff that happened today into only a few pages. I have just re-read it with a view to expand it, but decided it was ok as it is.

Tell a lie. I just went back and put the Feeder bit in. Just felt right.

Semi tangent-repeat: If you've never tried the jumping around to a kick-ass track thing; do it.
It's fucking brilliant. Such a release. (Chrissy's words)

The Feeder song works perfectly, if you need

ideas...

DAY 11

Thursday, 27th of March.

I woke to my alarm going off. Wow, that was a first. I usually wake up well before the alarm. Yesterday must have been good. Oh yeah, it had been. For all the right reasons.
I went down and found Chrissy sat at the kitchen table, in her running gear. "Bout time you showed up" she said "Been sat here for a while"
"Sorry, I usually wake before the alarm" I mumbled, still waking up.
"Gimme 5" I said and ran up to get changed.

I got back downstairs within a few minutes, then realised I had just thrown my wet running shoes in the corner the other day. Shit. I hoped they were dry. They weren't, and they were stinking.
"Jesus, time for new shoes" Chrissy said, turning away from the whiff.
"I don't really have much choice" I said putting the offending articles on my feet.
"We'll get you some when we get back" she said laughing "Come on"

We went out and did a 5k. I was struggling in my shitty shoes, but Chrissy aced it. No stopping, like a pro. I felt shit in comparison. And I was the runner! We clocked in at just over 28 minutes, but probably could have knocked time off if it wasn't for my shoes.

When we got back, she told me to "Put those hanging things in the bin!" before I entered the house. Wait, my house isn't it? Apparently not... I smiled.

My trusty shoes went in the bin, much to her relief. "I thought you were going to bring them in to wash them or something" she said in disgust.

"Nope. You're right. I'm going to treat myself to a new pair."

"Excellent. Baggsie the shower!" she shouted, running up the stairs.

I rolled my eyes, shook my head, and thought: what a woman.

While she did that, I got myself a new pair of trainers online. Asics Nimbus; my fav shoe (still is).

I also took the opportunity to get Chrissy a surprise to cheer her up. Well, hopefully. She didn't have a tracker watch, so I got her a Fenix like mine. Expensive morning, but worth it.

She came back down, and looked amazing as always. Just to make sure I noticed, she asked me. "I look ok?"

"You always look ok. Right now you look amazing"

Blush. She does it on purpose, I thought. Like she needs the affirmation. It was cute.

She kissed me "I've got to shoot, I'm meeting them at the café in a bit."

"Ok, hope it all goes ok"

She stepped back, and said "I love you. You know that right?"

"Trust me, I do" I said.

She smiled, turned, and left. Leaving a whiff of sweetness filling my nostrils. She smelled good.

I sighed contentedly, and went up to sort myself out.

Shower, change, coffee, work. I got stuck in.

I only had 2 short videos left to do, so I emailed a few clients to see if they had anything ready for next week. I got responses within an hour, with attachments. Another couple of short ones, and a long gear review. I took the short ones, and finished them by lunchtime.

Content, I shutdown, and went to make a sandwich. It was just before one, so I took my sarnie and ate it whilst walking over to the café.

Tinkle. Yes! Its back.

"Yeah, told you didn't I" Steve winked from behind the counter.

"Magic" I replied.

"Fuck you want?" he asked in his usual charming way.

"Nice. Nothing really, just came to say hi"

"Not even a coffee?" Willow piped up from behind

the coffee machine.

"Oh hi" I said, surprised "how was the course?"

"It was great. If you're injured whilst drinking coffee, I can save you" she laughed.

"Well if you're here, then I will have a coffee cheers. I try not to injure myself"

"Funny" She said. "Sit"

I went to my table, and Steve followed me over

"Oi, fuckface, who were the people Chrissy was with earlier? Were they Mary's kids?"

"Yeah, they've asked Chrissy to help make the arrangements and stuff"

"Ah, that's good of her."

"Fuckface?" I asked "That's a new one"

"Keeping it fresh mate" he said proudly.

"Dick"

"How have you been anyway? Everything ok?"

"Mate, I've had a couple of fantastic days. Perfect in fact. No negative thoughts, all good." I said, rather proud of myself.

"That's good to hear mate. Really is. You deserve to be happy"

"So do you mate. We both do."

"Like the two lost souls of Ramsey Forty Foot!" he said laughing.

"Something like that" I replied, laughing.

"What's so funny?" Willow asked, bringing my coffee over

"Just us two in general" I said.

"Couldn't agree more, pair of muppets" she laughed and walked off.

"Chrissy is an accountant right?" He asked
"Yeah, forensic accountant"
"What's the difference?" he asked
"Dunno" I shrugged my shoulders "Look it up. You need help?"
"You know me, I do my books, and it's all ok, but I just wanted a second opinion is all"
"I can ask if you like?"
"If you could. I don't want to, you know, be doing something wrong and stuff"
"Mate, I'll ask. I'm sure she won't mind."
"Cheers dude. You eating?" he asked
"No thanks mate, just had a sandwich. I really just popped in to see how things were"
"We are good mate. She's got us tickets to see Foo Fighters in June. She's amazing"
"Dude, that's fucking ace!" I said "You're a lucky guy. I'd love to see the Foos"
"Yeah, I am lucky. That's why I want to make sure I'm squeaky clean, you know"
"Mate, I'll speak to her tonight when she gets back. Will let you know"
"Effort, thanks"
"Right, I'm gonna go. I want to get home and tidy, make sure the place is ready for the kids."
"Sure, see ya later matey"
We hugged and I went back to the house.

House was cold and empty when I got back. I could quite easily have slipped into a depressive funk, but the thought of Chrissy staying here saved me.

She has the power to save me even when she's not here. What a woman.
I put the heating on, and worked my way around the house, cleaning, dusting, and hoovering.
(Yeah I said it; hoovering. Get over it.)
Took an hour or so, but I was finally done. Everything was tidy. Washing was in the dryer, and all I had to do was a bit of ironing.
I got myself a beer form the fridge, put some music on, and set up the ironing board. Let's smash it.

Tangent;
Rare glimpse into the normality of everyday life. I cleaned. I did laundry. I did ironing. Just like all of you. Just doesn't make for glamorous writing is all.

Half hour later, the ironing was done and put away. I cracked another beer (don't worry, I'm not an alcoholic; it's alcohol free beer), and sat down with my phone. Nothing from Chrissy, she must be busy. Few from the kids, and mum checking in. I sent my replies, and did a time check. 15.48.
Wow, the day had flown by. I was hoping Chrissy would be home soon, I missed her. I wandered into the kitchen to see what I could fix for dinner. Looks like pasta. I started making the sauce. From scratch obviously, wink. Nothing special, just standard tomato sauce with mince and peppers.
I left the pan on a low heat, and tidied up. Done. What to do now? I thought. Erm. Erm. Erm.

Dunno.

Too late to make bread. Erm. Erm. Pffff. Tanks? Nope. PlayStation? No. Guitar? No. What then? Shrug. My God, this was going nowhere. I called mum. Always good for a chat. She didn't disappoint; 38 minutes later, my ear on fire, I hung up. I had promised to talk to Chrissy about Chico; they really wanted him & had their hearts set on it. I could only do my best.

I went back to the kitchen and stirred the sauce. Still nothing from Chrissy. I hope everything was ok.

I set the table, ready for when she came home. *Proper little housewife aren't you Jackie boy!?* Oh fuck off will you. I just want her to feel at home. My phone rang, I answered "Hey mum, you forget something?"

"Mum? Try again lover boy"

"Hey!" instant happiness "How's it going? You going to be late?"

"All done, we've just got back from the solicitors. On way home, thought I'd check in"

"You sound happy, I take it things went ok?" I asked

"Yeah, they did. Better than ok. I'll be home in a bit, will tell you all"

"Ok, see you in a mo" I said and called off.

I was happy. Happy that she was happy. I was worried she may come home drained and upset, but it seems the opposite was true. I put the pasta on the boil, got some wine glasses, and poured us

a glass each. A minute or so later, the front door opened. The sweet, delicious smell of her perfume filled the room. My god it was good having her here. She came in and came straight over for a hug.
"My life, what a day. I'm pooped"
"I'm glad it all went well. Sit, I'll dish up."
She sat, and started telling me about her day. I served the food, and we carried on chatting about her day. "So there were no issues with the register office, they were really very good." She took a sip of wine. "And then we drove over to the solicitors in the city. I asked them again if they were sure they didn't want to do this with just the two of them, but they kind of insisted I come in with them I thought it was a bit weird, you know?" I nodded.
"Anyways, the solicitor got the will out and started reading. All monies form accounts and jewellery to be divided between the two children." She stopped and sipped her wine, then continued "then it came to the house." pause.
"Yes? And? I asked? Do they need to sell it?" I asked
"No, no sale required. Unless you want me to?" she hinted. I missed the point.
"What?" confusion.
"She left the house minus contents to me."
Silence
"What?" I asked, confused.
"She left the house to me Jack. It's mine to do with as I please. Mortgage free."
"And her kids were ok with that?" I asked incredulously

"Yes. The monies form accounts add up to a substantial sum. They are happy. And selling the house would just be a major hassle. They are more than happy that I got it. They actually signed the change to the will last year."

"Wow, that's... amazing." I said

"But?" she asked

"No, no but. I'm just surprised. No that's the wrong word. Let's face it, you have looked after her for some years now. I'm surprised by the news. If that makes sense" Duh, dickhead. What are you saying??

"You're funny. The said the same, and thanked me for looking after their mother. I signed the papers, it's all official."

"Well, that deserves a cheers" I said, and we clinked glasses. "What about the dog?"

"Ah, yeah, well. Hmmm. We asked the neighbour, and he couldn't have him because he goes to Spain for a few months every year. I really don't know what to do" She said

"Well, depending on the reward, I may be able to help..." I suggested.

"Reward? Jack Beckett! What kind of girl do you think I am??" she fluttered her eyelashes. Oh my God. Stop. Take a breath Jack!

"No, I erm, I didn't mean it like that. You know, I meant..."

"I love you, my tongue-tied stud" she said giggling. "You're funny when you get all mixed up"

"Well, I suppose this would be an occasion for me

to punch your shoulder....." I said.

"No!" she got up and I chased her around the table "Stop! No!" I grabbed her, and she continued her protests. "I have you now" I said sternly.

"Oh Sir, please be gentle" she giggled.

"You're mad" I said, letting her go. "Lovely, but mad"

Cue punch to shoulder

"Ouch! Wtf?"

"I'm not mad Jack Beckett. According to you I'm perfect" she said playing with her hair seductively.

"Oh my God, please stop" I pleaded "You're killing me here"

"Weirdo. What about the dog?"

"What? Oh yeah. The dog. Good subject change Missy." She bowed in agreement

"My folks want him. Like badly. My mum keeps going on about it"

"They do? That's great!" she smiled broadly. "We get to see him, and he's going to a great home"

"Yeah, they'll spoil him like crazy" I said

"Oh Jack, it's all coming together" she hugged me tight "I'm so happy"

"Me too Christelle Lenoir. Me too"

We sat back down, and I poured some more wine.

"What are you going to do with the house?" I asked

"Well, it should be empty by end of Monday. I could sell it. I could rent it out. I dunno. What do you think?"

"I have no idea" I said. "It's completely up to you"

"Maybe we should just clean and decorate it for

now. Then decide later"

"Good idea, would give us something to do in the evenings" I offered

"Cool. We'll go for a look around on Monday, and see what needs doing"

"I'll call mum and tell her about Chico" I said.

"Can I do it?" she asked

"Of course" I dialled mum and handed over the phone.

"Hi Barbara, its Chrissy. How are you? Yeah, I'm good thanks. Reason I'm calling is about Chico. Jack said you might be interested in taking him on? Yeah, aha, hmm. Yeah, ok. Well, nobody else seems to want him, so he's yours if you want him." I could hear mum shouting from where I was stood. It was pure joy. Chrissy giggled "I think she's happy" she said quietly

"Yes, I'm still here. When? Oh, erm, I can pick him up in the morning and bring him over if that's ok? About 10? Perfect. Ok Barbara, yep, ok, goodnight. Bye"

She hung up and handed me the phone. "She like to talk" I said.

"Yeah, I get that" she said exasperated. "But I'm happy they're taking him. She sounded so happy"

"You sure know how to make people happy" I said.

"I seems so" she winked.

"Oh stop!" I half shouted in frustration. "You're driving me mad"

"Sorry, I'll be a good girl from now on" Oh my God. Steady.

"Why don't you go have a cold shower while I tidy away the dishes" I suggested "Might cool you down a bit"

Giggles "Oh ok Jack, I'll go have a shower. Me. In the shower…."

"Fucking stop already!" I shouted laughing "Get away from me you foul vixen!"

"Whatever you say sir…." She ran her fingers across the wall as she walked away.

I took a deep breath. Chill Jack, chill. And…relax. Ok, get the dishes done, take your mind of her. In the shower. Fuck Stop! Grrrr!

I busied myself with the tidying, and calmed myself down.

What a woman.

I've said it a lot. But it's true. Still is all these years later. She's a natural flirt, only with me of course, but my God. I love it.

Anyhoo. Erm. Story. Yeah, let's put Jack in front of the telly, watching some crap whilst she gets her pj's on and joins him. And…….action!

"Hey, cooled down a bit have we?" I asked as she plonked down next to me on the sofa.

"Yes, sorry, I got a bit carried away. It's not fair. I'm just so happy"

"It's cool. I managed to calm myself down. You're not in danger anymore" I winked.

"Ooh Mr Darcy! Danger!" she fanned her face with her hands mockingly

"Stop it...." I said sternly

"Sorry" she giggled. "You're right. Let's be mature about this. Ahem... So Jack Beckett, how was your day?"

"Oh, nice change of subject" I said, nodding approvingly "Me? Well..."

I told her about my day, not much to tell really I guess, but she listened intently regardless.

She was giggling when I finished. "What's so funny?" I asked

"Fuckface" giggles "Where does he get this stuff from?"

"Yeah, he was trying to, and I quote, keep it fresh."

"He's funny" she smiled, keeping giggles under control. Just about.

"A true comedian" I noted. "Are you done giggling?"

"Yes. Sorry." Deep breath...and more giggling "No....sorry...."

I rolled my eyes "My God, what's wrong with you?"

"I...don't....know..." she managed between giggles. Jesus.

The Giggles. Wow. We've all been there right? I used to get them often, not quite so much following the divorce, but still, occasionally. If you haven't then you'll just have to imagine a woman, laughing/giggling uncontrollably. Literally. To the point of tears from laughing so much. Surely you've either done it or seen it??

Back in the room...

She eventually got herself under control, and the giggles subsided. Slowly. When she was done, she had tears running down her face and stomach muscle pain. Idiot.
We went to be happy. Again. I could get used to this.

Now, if you would excuse me, Sherlock is about to tear someone apart with deductive reasoning. I love it when he does that.

DAY 12

Thursday, 28th of March.

If I may, before we start: Questions I imagine readers have when reading this book.

1. Jack, when do you get paid?
Traditionally, people get paid at the end of the month, I get paid when clients were happy with the product, so basically weekly.

2. A lot has happened in a few days Jack, are you full of shit or did this actually happen?
Not being funny, dear reader, but I chose these 17 days for that precise reason; a lot happened in a short time-frame. Yes, it all happened. Seems far-fetched, but it did. We all have periods in our lives when a lot happens in a short time. This is one of those periods.

3. You seriously not going to sleep with her in this book?
No. sorry. Like I said, it's not that kind of book. You may be reading this seeing all the moments they have where it could easily go further, but it

aint gonna happen. You read a couple of chapters where I'm happy. Really happy. That can change in an instant. Unless you've been there, you wouldn't understand. I want to, believe me, but I'm not there. Talking about it with my wife recently because of this book, we agreed it was a long wait. But, well worth it. When it happened, it was fantastic, great, beautiful, all those things.

4. Ramsey Forty Foot. Seriously? Wtf? Hey, it's a real place, check it. Author speaking: I needed somewhere where I hadn't been. Where nobody has been (nobody I know). Somewhere with a canal. Random, but the whole tow-path thing was already in my head from the outset.
I looked on the map, and this place fit the bill. End of.

5. You seem to drink a lot of coffee. Are you ok? Yes thanks, I am. I drink about 3 or 4 coffees a day, didn't think that was weird or excessive.

6. You never give a lot of detail about the work you do, why not? My methods are secret. Author speaking again: I know nothing about content editing, it just needed a job that meant Jack worked from home. I watch a lot of YouTube vids about guitars, music, and gaming. So, I created my very own content editor. I wasn't going to research it so I could add loads of detail, as that isn't the focus of this story. The relationships and mental health are the story. (And yeah, I picked Forensic Accountant

at random too) I could easily go back and pad out the pages with useless info and drivel and make the book longer, but that's not what I want. I want to focus on Jack's life, mind, and the people around him. If that means I miss out on adding another 100 pages, so be it. My book, my choice.

If you think of any other questions, feel free to email me.
Back to the story.

I woke 2 minutes before the alarm. Not actually sure why I'd even set an alarm; I didn't have a lot to do today, so could afford to sleep in. But, I was/am a creature of habit. What day was it? Thursday. Kids won't be here till tomorrow. Got up, looked out the window. Rain. Shit. I hate grey, dismal, rainy days. It feeds depression. I was immediately on edge. I needed to take steps to stay positive today. *Too late you fucking loser! I'm in charge today.*
Fuck. No, not today. *Yes today. Get back in bed you piece of crap.* But I'm not... *Shut up. You're nothing. You're shit. Nobody really likes you, they all just feel sorry for you.* What? No they don't. Do they? *Think about it, everyone you know asking how you're doing, if you're ok. They know Jack, they know you're a fucking mess.* They don't... do they? Shit. I *am* fucked up. *Yes, you are. Now get back in bed you fucking loser.* Like a plane out of control, I was spinning downwards, about to crash. I couldn't stop it. I knew my tablets would help, but they were downstairs. I couldn't move. I could only

lay down. I curled up on the bed and pulled the duvet over me. It was warm, and dark. It felt safer than out there. *Good lad. Now, it's time to open the floodgates. Go on cry-baby.* I wept like a child, shaking, scared, alone in the dark. I was so disappointed with myself. I was letting everyone down. Again. Those thoughts only made it worse. *You are letting everyone down Jack. You always do. Your wife, your kids, your friends and family. Everyone. They all feel sorry for you because you're a fucking loser.* Eventually, the world went dark, inner voice subsided, and I was out.

I woke to find Chrissy in bed with me, holding me close. "Hey, what happened?" she asked.
"I'm so sorry" I muttered.
"You don't have to be sorry with me. I'm here for you Jack. I'm here" she was stroking my head. I realised I was holding her tightly. Too tight. I relaxed my hold, and apologised again. "Shhhh, it's ok. It's all ok. Tell me what happened"
I composed myself and told her about the inner voice. She listened intently, and didn't judge.
"Today, Mr Beckett, we are going to find you someone to talk to. Ok?"
I agreed, and fell asleep. She left me to sleep for another hour, then woke me. "Here, I brought you a coffee. And this" she handed me a pill. "Take it, lease?"
I did as I was told. "Good, now get yourself ready, and we'll find you someone to talk to."

Must have stood in the shower for ages, because there was a knock on the door followed by "You ok in there?"

"Yes thanks, be out now" I got out, dried off, and got myself dressed. I went down, and Chrissy did me some toast. "Ok, I've had a quick look, and there's a lady over in Chatteris that looks perfect. I spoke to her, and she can fit you in on Monday. No choice here Jack" she looked at me, waiting for me to argue.

"No argument. Thank you" I said.

"Good" smiles

"I love you" I said

"I love you too" she replied, and kissed me.

The smell of her perfume helped to lift me. Sweet as a summers' day.

"Question?" I said

"Hmmm?"

"What are those?" I motioned over to a stack of boxes by the back door. A large stack. A lot of boxes.

"Plants" she beamed. "How about a gardening day?"

"Sounds great"

"You taking the piss?" she asked

"No, no. Sorry. I mean it. It will be good to keep busy today" I explained

"Super!" she smiled "There's enough there to keep us going all day"

Great. I mean literally, great. I'm not a gardener, but keeping busy is what I needed, so I was happy.

After breakfast, we went out back, and she laid out her grandiose plan for the garden. It did involve a lot of work. The rain had stopped half hour or so ago. Good. "Let's get stuck in" I said.

And we did.

Just after midday, I stopped. "Oi, let's take a break eh?" I said, knackered and muddy.

"Yeah, good idea". She looked equally knackered.

We washed up and I suggested we go to the caff for lunch. "Yes please, I could do with a good coffee"

"Me too, I 'm sick of being wet and cold" I winked.

The caff was busy when we got there, lunchtime rush in full swing. We weren't planning on staying, so joined the queue. When we eventually got to the front, Steve saw us and said "Why the fuck you queueing with the plebs?"

"Good afternoon to you too Stephen" Chrissy said, giggling.

"Hello, Madame, how may I be of service?" he smiled "Better?"

"Madame? What? No fuckface today?" I asked.

He looked embarrassed "Whatever knobby. What you want?"

Chrissy giggled "You crack me up"

"Glad to be of service" he bowed.

"Ignore him" Willow said "Good to see you guys. What can I get for you?"

"Hey" Chrissy smiled "Just two latte's please to take out"

"Coming up"

I looked at Steve "You got and decent sarnies left?"
"Decent? I'll have you know they're all decent you prick"
I could hear giggling behind me. The ladies did love a bit of Steve.
"Ploughman's and..?" I looked at Chrissy
"I'll have the same"
"Two ploughman's please kind sir"
"Your wish, is my command" Steve bowed and went out to the kitchen.
He returned with two massive looking sandwiches. "Here you go Madame. Is there anything else I can get for you?"
"No thank you Sir."
"Splendid. If Sir could possibly provide a form of payment?" he looked at me
"Of course." I tapped the thing and made my contactless payment
"Makes a fucking change" Steve mumbled
"Pardon?" I asked
"Thank you Sir"
"No, thank you. These sandwiches look great" I said
"Don't overplay it dickwad, fuck off out of here"
More giggles from Chrissy. "Bye Stephen. See you later Willow, thank you"
"Cheers guys, have a good day" Willow called.
I winked at Steve and we left.
"He's funny" she said as we walked home
"Every inch the ladies' man" I commented
She spat out her coffee, laughing

"Get your mind out of the gutter Lenoir"
"Sorry" she laughed
We made it home without further coffee spitting incidents thankfully, and sat at the kitchen table to eat our sarnies.

"You're very lucky" she said between bites
"Hmmm?" I mumbled, mouth full of food. Lucky? To have her? Of course I was.
"To have Steve in your life" she replied "And me, of course"
"Yes, he's a good friend." I said. Where was this going?
"Wish I had a Steve in my life" she said
"Hmmm???" I managed, mouth refilled.
"No, not like that. I meant a best friend"
I swallowed "I'm sure you have plenty of friends"
"Erm. No actually. I don't" she suddenly looked sad
"What? Surely…" but she cut me off.
"After my parents died, I withdrew completely, and lost all my friends. I made a few friends in Uni, they all moved away after graduation, so I was left on my own again."
A tale very similar to my own I thought. "What about your sister?" I asked "I thought you mentioned a sister"
"Fleur lives in Boston, she moved there after graduating from medical school. I see her once every few years. She has her own family to worry about now, so we don't speak very much. I think it reminds her of mum and dad, and she just wants

to put that behind her"

"Wow, that's pretty harsh" I said.

"We were never really close to be honest, she's older than me and always resented all the attention I got as the youngest."

"That must be tough. I can't compare, I'm an only child"

"That's how I see myself now." eyes drawn.

"Surely you made friends through work?" I asked

"I work from home Jack. There's a reason for that. I did it to protect myself."

"But you seem a natural at it, I've seen you with Willow"

"I'm getting there" she started, but I must have been thinking out loud

"Protect yourself?"

"Work wasn't a good experience for me"

"What happened?" I asked

"I met someone at work, he seemed really nice. We went out a few times, and then, you know, slept together"

Uncomfortable, but not unusual Jack, she had a life before you. But all I could manage was "Ok..."

"Then he started telling all his friends in the office how it was, how I was in bed. You know. It was like he'd done it as a dare or something. I was devastated"

"What a bastard" I said, my anger rising.

She noticed and quickly added "It's all behind me now Jack. I was so embarrassed, I left. And that's why I started working for myself. Safely at home."

Things started clicking into place in my head. The delay in sleeping with me, mentioning we both had issues to work through. Fuck. It all made sense now.

"I'm not like that" I blurted out before I could stop myself.

"Hey" she took my hand "I know you're not. Believe me, I do. But I'm just not ready right now. Does that make sense?"

"Perfect sense" I said. "I'm sorry you had to go through all that, but I'm glad you told me. It kind of explains stuff, you know?"

"I do. And thank you. You notice I don't cry or show emotion over it?" she asked

"Yes…"

"I'm done crying over it. Each time I cried, he won. So, I stopped enabling his victories. I'm numb to it now"

Wow, I thought. How do I get to that point??

"Do me a favour?" she asked

"What?"

"Can we not talk about it again? I'm kind of keen to stay away from the subject." she asked

"Of course, there's no need to talk about it again." I re-assured her

"Thank you." She finished her sarnie. "Ready to get back out there?"

"You bet. We have 2 hours till the kids get here" I said, and we went back out into the garden.

The rain was still holding off, so we managed to get a lot done before it was time to call it a day.

We cleared up, had showers, and got ready for the kids to come home. Yes, that's right; home. Like I said before; they live with their mother, but this is their Home.

"You happy with your garden?" I asked, as we had a cup of tea out on the deck

"My garden?" she asked

"All yours. Unless you plan on going somewhere?" I said

"No, I think I'm home" she said. "I think I'm finally home"

She had no way of knowing of course, but she *was* home. And she wouldn't be going anywhere; she's still here now, all these years later, sat out on the deck with a G&T whilst I type this.

Quick tangent?

Just a quick one about Chrissy's revelation. What would you have done? Would you have handled that differently? I really like what she said about not letting him win anymore, and being able to be numb towards a situation like that. I really did hope I would get to that point too. Years later, I kind of am, but it only takes a little thing to bring it all back. But that's a different tangent. This one is about her, not me. I would never have thought that about her, she's so confident, outgoing, and will talk to anyone. Where does that come from? I certainly don't have those skills. Was it all just repressed and now suddenly released upon an unsuspecting world? Who knows? Who cares? I'm glad she had started to be more open, or accessible, whatever you want to call it. It was working. She'd impressed my kids, my parents, my friends. It was all good. She was the outgoing kind that I needed to drag me out of my shell. Would never really happen like that, but we did get out a lot. Far more than I would have on my own.

We never spoke about the incident again, and I never got the feeling that she distrusted me. The Florence trip was the big one for us, we knew after that we spend the rest of our lives together.

But I digress…. Tangential tangent.

Doorbell…

Chrissy opens door; kids come running in with hugs for all. She was right, I thought, she is home.

"Hey guys" all smiles. She really is finally home. You know those moments when you get so happy, you get a tear in your eye? No? You ain't old enough/don't have kids. It you know; this was one of those moments. I was so stupidly happy to see the acceptance, it brought a tear to my eye. Elsie was all over her, telling her about school, her friends, her hair, al that girlie stuff. She's never really done that with her mother. Don't know why, didn't care. James was a bit more restrained, not in a bad way, I just think he was a bit shy around her. Remembering what he'd said; "She's tidy dad…" I rolled my eyes. Teenagers eh.

After ten or so minutes of chit chatting about all things school, football, hair, and friends, they retreated to their lairs.

Oh, before I forget, and you get any ideas; we'd discussed sleeping arrangements earlier this afternoon. Chrissy would be in my room, and I set up an airbed in the office. She was against it, but I told her I didn't trust myself around her, so sleeping together would be bad. (Insert shoulder punch here) Besides, she had nowhere else to go. It worked, and I really didn't mind.

"They're amazing" she said, smiling. "Such loving kids"
"Take after their father" I said. "Their mother is a cold-hearted, unloving bitch" (ok, so I didn't actually say that last bit, but I did think it)
"Yes, they do" she said, looking me in the eye. What?
"What?" I asked.
"Just looking"
My turn to blush.
"Oh my Mr Beckett, I do believe you're blushing" she said, fluttering her eyelashes.
"Stop it Lenoir" I warned her
"Or what?" she asked, teasingly.
My eyes widened "Or what???" I grabbed her and started tickling "I'll give you 'or what' Missy!"
It was a fun moment, we both laughed a lot. I liked seeing her happy, I thought, it's comforting. And it makes *me* happy.
I started getting things out to make dinner, and she said "Hey, I'll do it"

I said "you sure? I'm just doing spag-bol"
She looked at me and said "I want to. Please?"
"Ok, all yours" I surrendered. "Can I at least make bread?"
"That's one thing I can't do, so please do" she said.
"Deal"

Minor notey thing: Her insistence on making dinner will be explained tomorrow. Be patient.

I think I got the better end of the deal; I had frozen baguettes in the freezer. "Hey! What the hell are those?" she asked
"Bread?" I said, "I was just going to put them in the oven?"
"You bugger! You said you were making bread!"
"I did? Maybe I said baking bread, not making?"
I just failed to avoid the tomato flung at me, and it hit me on the chest, leaving a mess on my t shirt.
"Aaaah! Hey!" I shouted
"Oh shit!" she said, hand to her mouth "I'm sorry"
"Hmmm. Nice one Lenoir" I said "I'll have to change out of this mess"
"Feel free to change here" wink.
"I think I'll go upstairs if it's all the same with you" I said
"Your loss" she said
"You!!!" I said, clenching my fists with all the frustration I could muster
Giggles.
"You're such a freakin tease!" I said, walking out of the kitchen.

"Love you too!" she shouted after me.
What a woman.

I came back, fresh shirt on, and found my two ladies in conversation in the kitchen. Elsie was helping out. Wait. Helping out? She never offered to help *me* out!
"What happened to your shirt dad?" she asked
"Oh, just an accident" I said, glaring at Chrissy
She flashed me a gorgeous smile. Fuck. I could never be angry at this woman I thought. Look at her. Man alive…
I resumed my task, and put the baguettes in the oven.
"How are we getting on?" I asked, walking over to the ladies
"I'm helping" Elsie said proudly
I kissed her head "That's great sweetheart"
"What the Fuck?" I mouthed to Chrissy, perplexed. She just laughed and shrugged her shoulders.
"She's doing a superb job, aren't you?" she said shoulder bumping Elsie, who smiled broadly.
"Looks like it! You're a great helper Ello" I ruffled her hair
"Hey!" she protested.
"I'll set the table. Wait, no I won't" I had a better idea "James!" I shouted "Set the table please mate!"
Elsie started laughing "Oh daddy, he'll never do that! She said
She was wrong. He came down, and set the table without arguing.

Again, I looked at Chrissy and mouthed "What the fuck?"

She just laughed. Again. What was going on here? Ugh, wait. I think I knew. "She's tidy dad" played in my head again. Seriously? He's doing this because Chrissy is fit? *Yeah, makes sense eh Jackie boy, he's a teenage lad.* Yeah. Again, I'd have to agree with you on that. Christ.

"Thanks bud" I said, awestruck

"No probs dad" he said, sitting down. "You need any help Chrissy?"

Oh fuck right off. Seriously? What the fuck has happened to my children??

"No thank you James, we have it all in hand. Don't we Ello?"

"Yes James, it's all under control" Elsie said, pretending to be grown up.

James shrugged, pulled out his phone, and started texting.

Wait. Did you hear that? Nah. No, actually yes, I did. She said Ello. *That's your nickname Jack! She's taking over.* Don't be fucking stupid, she's just blending in, and it's a good thing. It sounded so natural, and neither of the kids batted an eyelid. *Ok, I'll give you that one.*

The oven beeped, so I took the bread out and put it on the table.

"Good timing. Sit down you lot, I'll bring the food over" Chrissy said.

We all sat, and had a fantastic family meal. I say that, and I mean it. Family. We felt like a family.

Again, it will become clearer tomorrow.

"Right boys, you're on dishes duty" Chrissy announced when we'd all finished. Again, zero protest from James. What the actual...? Whatever. We cleared up and did the dishes, talking about football. He has football practice tomorrow, and was super excited. It had been cancelled for ages now due to the snow. But, the snow had all but gone, and the pitches were accessible.

After we'd finished, we joined the girls in the living room, and watched tv for a while. The kids eventually did that thing where they quietly disappear up to their rooms to do whatever it is they do. I told James he could go on the PlayStation till 10, and let Elsie have her phone.

"Thank you for dinner" I said, cosying up to Chrissy "It was lovely."

"How good were the kids though eh? What the hell is going on there?" she said

"Well, Elsie obviously loves you. And James...well, erm, you know, he's a teenage boy, and you're an attractive female"

She laughed "Get out of it! You serious?"

"Yeah, after he first met you he told me 'She's tidy dad, you did well' ".

"Tidy? Wow, I'm honoured." she laughed "Bless him, that's lovely"

"I was a bit worried, but he's just a teenage lad I guess"

"Yeah, but with good taste, like his dad" she

winked.
"Wouldn't go that far" I said
Shoulder punch "Ouch!"
"Dick"
Another shoulder punch
"What the hell??"
"That's for calling me an attractive female" she said
"What?"
"Dunno" she giggled
We watched a bit of Gogglebox before calling it a night. Love a bit of Gogglebox.
After checking on the kids, we went to our separate rooms. Well, she did, I went to my airbed in the flippin office.
Headphones deffo required tonight; this was not going to be a good night's sleep.

Ah Beckett! There you are. Come along, the game's afoot!

Night.

DAY 13

Friday, 29th of March.

Oh my God. What a shit nights' sleep. The bloody airbed has a leak, I had to pump it up about 6 times during the night. I was not in a great mood, and my back hurt. I got my phone out and bought a new one straight away, though won't be delivered till tomorrow. So, one more night of this. Fuck sake.

I looked at my watch; 06.02. Fucking hell. I took my sleeping bag and went down stairs to lay on the sofa. Wide awake. Tired. Shit.

"Hey, thought I heard you, you ok?"

I shit myself. She's like a fookin ninja.

"Jesus! Erm, yeah, didn't sleep too good, and wide awake."

"Go up to your bed and get comfy" she said "I'll make tea"

I did as I was told, and curled up in the warm bed. It smelled of her. It felt like heaven.

She came up a few minutes later with two steaming cups of tea. "Scoot up"

I moved over a bit (to the cold part) and let her

in. She cuddled into me, and we just lay there. No words spoken. Just lying there, feeling the warmth and comfort of each other's bodies. It was pure bliss.

Needless to say, the tea went untouched. I woke a while later, and checked the alarm clock; 08.14. Wow. I felt great. Chrissy was curled up next to me, still asleep. Hair across her face, her eyes shut. Totally peaceful and beautiful. *You're so lucky Jack.* Yeah, I know.

I sat there watching her until she woke and flashed those beautiful green eyes at me.

"Morning" she smiled.

"Morning yourself." I said

"You been awake long?" she asked

"For a bit. Just been sat her watching you"

"Pervert" she teased

"Nothing like that Lenoir, just looking and thinking how lucky I am"

"Weirdo"

"Lucky weirdo, thank you"

"Whatever" she reached over to get her tea

"It's freezing" I said

"Ugh, yeah, it is. Wow, we been here for w awhile? What time is it?"

"Almost twenty past eight"

"Ooh, nice lay in. I was out like a light." she yawned

"Me too. Thank you"

"For what?"

"For letting me in. I need you to know that I wouldn't ever try anything on without your say-so. You shouldn't ever worry about that"

"I know that" she said, sipping cold tea "Ugh, that's horrible."

"You want to shower first?" I asked

"Nope, I want to lay here for a bit, you go"

I got up, and left her there, blissfully spread out in the bed. I showered, dressed, and went down to make the kids breakfast.

2 things worth exploring here I think:

1. Sleeping with your partner. Studies have shown that you sleep easier and better when laying with the person you love. If you doubt it consider:
   - How badly did you sleep after your partner left you?
   - How badly do you sleep if you're apart? Say you're away with work or something in a hotel. I sleep very badly, and the wife the same.

It's a weird thing. Studies show that it improves couple bonding. What? Yes, think about it; whenever I get home from a trip, I can't wait to go to bed with my wife. Not in THAT way necessarily, but just to feel her next to me. It's weird how that works. I know I'm not talking rubbish, because it's been proven. Some may also call it separation anxiety. Whatever it is, it's a thing. You can tell from the last paragraph above that we both slept deep when we were together; 2 hours went by in the blink of an eye, and we both woke happy.

2. Making your kids breakfast. Really? You're kids are old enough now surely. Doesn't matter. I love making my kids food. It's an absolute joy to see them enjoying a meal. I still do it now. I love it.

On with the story...

The kids emerged from their beds about 40 minutes later. I had a stack of pancakes ready in the oven, and the table was set. "Morning guys" I kissed each of their heads. "Have a seat, I have breakfast" I got them both a glass of milk, and put the plate of pancakes on the table.
"Yes! Get in. Effort dad" James said, his sleepy mood instantly gone.
"Ooh pancakes, yeay!" Elsie was equally happy. Which made me happy.
I made a coffee, and sat watching them eat. It was bliss.
Chrissy came down, her hair tied up, still wet. "Something smells good"
"Dad made pancakes" Elsie beamed
"There's enough if you want some" James added.
"Ooh, yes please" she pulled out a chair, and joined us.
"I'll get you a coffee" I said, and stood to get one.
I stood watching them as I made the coffee, it was a picture of family awesomeness; two happy kids, with a happy... Happy what? What do they call her? She's nothing to them relation wise. Hmmm. She would obviously eventually become their step-

mum, but they always called her Chrissy, and still do.

I gave Chrissy her coffee, and sat back down. What a fantastic start to the day. I wished it could last forever. We talked about what we would do today; Elsie wanted to go to her friend's house later on, and James had football basically most of the afternoon. Tomorrow? Don't know yet, we'll have a think. The kids helped tidy up after, and Chrissy went up to dry her hair.

When teeth were brushed, and hair sorted out, we all went for a walk. They weather was playing nice; it was dry, and the puddles had mostly gone. About ten minutes into our walk, I could hear it coming; Chico came lumbering out from some bushes, my parents not far behind. The kids were made up; they didn't know mum and dad had taken him over, and were ecstatic. They'd always wanted a dog, but as parents, we'd been against it. Mum and dad looked happy. It was good to see them out and about. Don't get me wrong, neither of them were ill or impaired in any way, but they just didn't really go out for walks unless I dragged them out.

They were also happy to see the kids. Big hugs and kisses all round. Could life get any more perfect? I thought. Probably not.

We joined the parents, and walked a good 4k or so. There was lots of chatting going on, stick throwing, and general fun being had. When we got back to our house, the kids begged mum and dad to come in, but they were tired and wanted to go home. "Hey guys, why don't we let Nan and grandad go home and chill. You've both got to go soon anyway" I reminded them. Disappointment from the kids, thankful looks from the parents. Sorted.

We said bye, and went inside. "You guys want lunch before you go?" I asked. James would get something at the footie club, and Elsie was having lunch at her friend's house. "Ok guys, go get your stuff and I'll drop you off" The kids ran upstairs to sort their stuff out, and then we drove them to wherever they needed to be.

After dropping them off, I sat in the car with Chrissy. "Well, what now?" I asked.

"Lunch?" she suggested. I looked at the clock, it was just after twelve.

"Good idea. Where?"

"There's a nice coffee place in Ramsey" she suggested.

Bit weird, why not Steve's? I thought. Oh well. "Yeah, sure, let's go"

We drove the short distance to the village centre, parked up, and walked to the café.

The place was empty. Obviously not as good as Steve's place. She sat at a table right in a corner, away from the counter. What's going on? We looked through the menu, and ordered food and drink at the counter.

"So, what's going on?" I asked. "Why this place?"

"I lied. It's not a great place, and I knew it would be

empty." she whispered.

"Ah, ok. But, why?"

"I wanted us to be able to talk without distractions" she said

Suspect. What is happening here??

"Don't worry, it's nothing disastrous. I just wanted to talk to you about the kids"

My heart sank, and my stomach dropped. I think she could see. "Oh hey, nothing bad, I just wanted to tell you something"

"Right..." I said, worried regardless.

The girl came over with our order, and we thanked her.

"I wanted to talk about me and the kids" she started "Not sure if I'm going to word this right, so please bear with me"

"Ok..." I said

"Right. So. I'm beyond the age of having kids of my own. I know that. And it hurts. I'm not going to sugar coat it, it hurts bad. It's like a part of me is missing. But, I've accepted the fact that it's too late now." She could see I was about to counter, so continued "I know women have kids well into their 40s, I know that. My issue is not with being an old mum, it's with me. I have premature ovarian failure." she looked at me, expectantly.

"I have a vague idea of what that means, but I'd be guessing" I said.

"It usually happens to women in their early forties, very unusual for women in their thirties" She said "I must be very unusual."

"I'm sorry" I said, holding her hand.

"No, really, I'm ok with it. I've accepted it. I found out last year, and it was tough for a while."

This woman was so incredibly resilient, I thought. How do I get to that place?

"Anyway, you're probably wondering how this relates to James and Elsie. I'm not going to lie to you Jack, and I need you to know something"

"What?" I asked

"I am in this relationship to the fullest extent I can be. I'm fully invested if you like. I get a good feeling from you Jack, and I think we have a long future together"

"I feel the same" I said

She leaned over and kissed me "That's exactly what I was hoping and expecting to hear" she said, relieved "So, the kids. I want to be more than your girlfriend to them Jack. I want to be more than a step mum, if it comes to that. I want to be everything for them. Don't get me wrong, I'm never going to be their mother. They have one already, and I could never come between them. I want to be as close to a mother as I can get though. Does that make sense?"

"Completely" I said

"I want to cook for them, do their washing, help them with homework, be a listening ear, love them, look after them. Basically like a mother, but not."

I thought for a moment, just to make her sweat, then said "You have no idea how happy it makes

me to hear that"
"You mean it?" I could see tears forming in her eyes
"No, not really"
"Wha…? Oh you!" she punched my shoulder (yet again!) "You're a dick."
"Ouch! I mean it, I couldn't possibly be happier." I said, rubbing my sore shoulder. This girl had a punch.
"Thank you" she leaned in and we kissed. "Thank you"
She wiped the tears from her eyes, and composed herself. "Gosh, I must look a state"
"Well, yeah, but still fit" I winked, covering my shoulder in anticipation.
"Oh you….you…."
"Yes….?"
"Fuckwad"
"Whoa, fuckwad?? You've been spending far too much time around Steve"
"Whatever" she laughed. We both laughed. We'd just weathered another storm. And come out the other side unscathed, and our relationship stronger.
"Can we get out of here and get a decent coffee now please?" I whispered
"Yeah, let's go" she replied, nodding.
I paid up, and we drove over to the Willow Tree Café, the home of most excellent coffee. And people.

Willow's coffee was infinitely better than what we

just had.

"The fuck you go there for?" Steve asked

"We were in the neighbourhood" I said.

"Hmmm. Still a dickhead. A lesser man would be hurt, but not me"

"Not even a little?" I asked

"I invite you to please fuck the fuck off" he said, looking all aloof

"Ooooooh, get you!" Chrissy said, leaned over and kissed him on the cheek

"Fuck sake girl, Willow's just over there!"

"Oh don't mind me" she said "You carry on"

"Wha....?" he looked dumbfounded "You're all fucking against me!" he said in mock despair

"Poor baby's feelings been hurt?" Willow said in a very condescending voice and gave him a hug. Chrissy and I laughed and went to my (I guess now OUR) usual table.

We enjoyed our coffees, had a chat about this and that, then said goodbye to the two lovebirds and went home. "I love those guys" Chrissy said smiling as we walked home.

"Yeah, they're great. Life would certainly be duller without them in it" I responded "You want me to see if they fancy a drink later?"

"Yeah, I'd like that"

I got my phone out and sent the text.

When we got home, I picked up the post, and saw there was a letter from Helen's solicitor. Instant alarm bells; Shields up! Red Alert!

"What is it?" Chrissy asked

"A letter from her solicitor" I said, quietly

"Can't be anything bad though can it? I thought everything had been sorted out already?"

She was right, it had already been finalised. What could this be? Stay positive Jack, stay positive.

Chrissy instinctively knew what was going on in my head. She took my hand and said "Hey, it's not going to be anything bad, ok?"

"Yeah, no it's not"

"But, only one way to find out…"

"Yes" I said and opened it.

Relief. And anger. Instant anger. The letter basically was requesting I sent a letter stating the specific details of the holiday, including dates of travel, any flight numbers, and address of accommodation, so a letter of authority could be provided.

"What the fuck…?" I muttered

"What is it?" she asked. I handed her the letter.

"I need a letter of authority to take my kids out of the country?" I asked, my voice tinged with anger.

"Relax Beckett, its standard stuff. My sister has a similar thing going on. She has legal custody, it's actually the law."

She was making sense, but I was still angry.

"The law is weird like that Jack. Usually, it's the other way around, because your kids have your surname. If she changes her name back, she will need one from you if she takes them out of the country as their names will be different. Make sense?"

"Yeah, I guess so" I did get it, she would need one from me too. Made sense. I calmed down.

"All good?" she asked

"Yeah, all good" I said, taking a deep breath. I relaxed. *It's all good Jacko*. Yes it is. Wait, why you on my side?? *Gotto sometimes boy innit.* Whatever, just behave please.

Ok, shields down Jack. And relax.

"How about a run?" Chrissy asked "Might help to clear your head"

"Great idea" I said. God knows I needed to clear my head right now, a run would do nicely.

"Hey" I said "That reminds me, I got you a present" I ran upstairs and retrieved the box.

"A present for me?" Flashes eyelashes.

"Yep, nothing special, just thought it would be nice" I said and handed her the box

She opened it and shrieked "Oh my God Jack! This is so cool! Thank you" She flew at me and showered me with kisses.

"Hey! Yo! Steady on!" I laughed

"You know, I've been thinking of getting one of these for a while" she said, admiring the new Fenix on her wrist.

"Got you a few funky coloured straps as well I said, handing her a package with Neon green, Purple, and Yellow watch straps in it.

"Oh wow! Awesome, I love purple, I love all of them" More kisses.

I changed the strap for her, and helped her set up

the watch, and pair it with the newly downloaded app on her phone. Done. Happy lady.

We got changed, and hit the streets. Well, towpath. Weather wasn't too bad, little bit of drizzle, but nothing heavy. The run was fantastic, there was minimal talking, maximum effort.

Time was pretty good, just over 27 mins. She was driving me to be better, which was just fantastic. To be honest, we drove each other. She had started pretty slow, with a lot of stopping, but now was running the 5k like a boss. And, besides, we were having fun, which was the most important bit. I had always thought running was a bit of a drag, just something I had to do. I enjoyed it, but never seemed to get that "Runners High" that people talk about. Until now. Running with Chrissy made it all better. *Anyway, enough of that, get back to the story Jack.* Oh yeah, sorry…

We got back, more sweaty than wet, but totally happy. A real runners high for once.

Showers, change. Cup of tea. "What's the plan for dinner tonight?" she asked "You want me to do something?"

"Well," I said "I thought I'd treat the kids to pizza express tonight. What you think?"

"There's a pizza express here?" she asked incredulously.

"No, it's down in Huntingdon."

"Ah. Ok, yeah, that would be cool" she said

"The kids love it there, might take their minds off

the horrors of the divorce" I said.

"You think it's on their minds?" she asked

"Well, I guess it would be wouldn't it? Suddenly living in a world where their parents are no longer together. Different homes. Must impact them right?"

"I guess you're right. Have you ever sat them down and talked about it?"

"You know, I have thought about it, but never actually gone through with it." I said pensively.

"You really should Jack, it's good to get feelings out in the open. Might provide them with some comfort too"

"Yeah, you're right. I'll give it a go."

"Tell you what, I have a bit of work to do tomorrow, I may go over to the cafe and work from there for a bit. Give you guys a bit of space, you know?"

"That's really nice of you" I said "are you sure?"

"Yeah, it will be good for all of you. For all of us. In the meantime, you have a bit of time to go over what you might say"

"I might actually do that, last thing I want to do is get it all wrong. Knowing my luck, it'll all come out wrong"

Oh shit! The kids! I grabbed my phone and checked for messages. Fortunately, there weren't any. I text them both to see how they were doing, and to make sure they got back here by five at the latest. Replies came almost instantaneously; concurrence and reassurance. Jack was going to pick Elsie up from her friend's house and they'd get the 1640 bus. Love them.

It was a couple of minutes to four; they'd be back in an hour or so. I busied myself tidying the house, whilst Chrissy sat ordering more plants, or whatever she was doing. She looked fully relaxed on the sofa, so I just left her to it.

A while later, both kids streamed in asking what was for dinner as apparently they were "Starving dad"!"

"Well, guys, I'm sorry, I forgot to get something for dinner" I said

"Dad!" moans, complaints

"Hey. Chill Tell you what. What don't we go to pizza express?"

"Yes!!" and other chants of teenage jubilation. "Ok, go get yourselves ready"

James ran off to have a shower, and Elsie just ran off to the sofa and sat with Chrissy, chatting about random girlie stuff no doubt.

It felt good to have a family around me again. Even if it was only for the weekend. *Can't have it all Jackie boy!* Nope, you're right; you can't.

My phone buzzed in my pocket. I took it out, and opened the message; Steve.

Him: Hey fucknut, what you guys doing for dinner?
Me: good timing knobby, we were about to leave to go to pizza express. Wanna join?"
Him: Give us ten.
Me: Roger that.

I went and told the guys the news, which was met with yet more teenage excitement; they loved Steve. Chrissy was also happy, she could have a good old gossip with Willow no doubt.
Ten minutes later, Steve and Willow joined us, and we all drove down to Huntingdon together. I was just hoping they had a table for all of us… Serves you right for not reserving a table dickhead. Yeah, ok, got it. But that would mean speaking to someone on the phone; an activity I liked to avoid as much as possible. As luck would have it, they had plenty of space, so we got a table easy enough.

Picture, if you will, the scene:
Super excited kids discussing what to have. Two ladies exchanging the latest gossip. Two best friends giving each other stick for random stuff. All in all a loving scene, picture perfect in fact.
We had a great night; dough balls, pizza, gelato, tiramisu, and fantastic company. It was fucking brilliant. All too soon, it was time to go home though. It saddened me to break up this scene of perfect bliss. But, we had to go home sometime right?
I paid the bill, much to Steve's protest, and we all went home. We said goodbye to Steve and Willow, leaving them with promises of coming to the caff for breakfast tomorrow. Everyone was happy. Result. I was happy. Result. Right? Yeah Jackie boy, result. *Well done matey, you really pulled it out of the bag tonight. BZ.* I had no idea what the fuck

was going on with my inner voice. Why was it being so nice? Had we turned a corner somewhere? Whatever. I wasn't going to argue. *You know I can hear you right, fuckwad?* Yeah, I do. Thank you. I really appreciate it.

"You ok?" Chrissy asked. I really hoped I hadn't said any of that out loud. Double check? No, you didn't. Thanks.

"Yeah, I was just thinking about how perfect tonight was" I said.

"Yeah, it really was, wasn't it?" she agreed.

We hugged, and went off to watch tv with the kids.

A great end to day 13 right? Ha! No unlucky 13 for us. It was a great day, and I was looking forward to far more days like it in the future. The kids went to bed happy.

When it was time for Chrissy and I to do the same, I kissed her goodnight, and went to go to my airbed in the office. I didn't care how shit it was, I was too happy to care.

"Hey. Beckett. Where do you think you're going?"

I turned "What? To bed?" I said, confused.

"Nope. You're in here. With me." she said.

"You sure?" I asked

"No funny business?" she asked

"No, no funny business"

"Then get in here" she said.

I wasn't about to complain.

I had one of the best nights' sleep I'd had in years.

No head phones, no Sherlock Holmes. Just the

warmth and sweet smell of the woman I loved.

Fuck me, it can't get better.

DAY 14

Saturday, 30th of March.

I've been sat here thinking for a while, but am still struggling to put into words how good it felt to wake up next to this beautiful, loving, caring, just overall fantastic woman. You'll just have to use your imagination.
Needless to say Jack Beckett was a happy boy when he woke up.

I lay for a while, just watching her sleep. Until…
"I can feel you watching me Beckett" eyes still closed.
"Tis witchcraft!" I said jokingly
"You calling me a witch??" instantly awake and on the defensive. All playful of course.
"I wouldn't dare" I said, and kissed her. "Good morning beautiful"
Even though she'd only just woken up, she still blushed.
"Morning" she said "I slept like, super well" she said, stretching.
"Yeah, me too. Best sleep I've had for ages."

"We're good together aren't we Jack?" she asked
"We are superb together." I assured her. "I couldn't imagine better"
We kissed, and rolled out of bed, onto the floor to much laughter.
"Get up you loon" she said. "We have a breakfast date to keep remember"
"Yep, gimme 5 and I'll be ready to go" I said, sprinting for the bathroom.
"Five?? I'll need more than that you prat!" she called after me.
It's funny how there is such a difference between men and women when it comes to getting ready in the morning. Depending on the situation I guess. In this case, we were going out, and it would take her a bit longer than usual to get ready, as she wanted to look "Her best". Women eh…

I was dressed and ready before she even got in the shower, so I had plenty of time to ensure the kids were ready to go. Needn't have worried; they were both already sat in the kitchen ready to go.
"Morning you two" I said "Bit keen aren't we?"
"Daddy, I'm hungry" Elsie said. "When can we go?"
"Chrissy will be ready in five or ten minutes" I said "Give her a bit of time"
James piped up "Yeah Elsie, be more patient will you?" Bless him, proper teenage crush. Defending his maiden. Funny. Right…?
Chrissy was ready a few minutes later. She came down, jeans, t-shirt, hair in a braid. Picture of

beauty, even at her most casual.

We made our way to the caff to feed the two hungry animals. We had trouble keeping up with them on the way over; they were basically running.

Tinkle.

"Hey you cretins!" came the greeting from Steve behind the counter "come over here and give me a hug" The kids ran over and gave the requested hug. Steve loved kids. Loved my kids. Should do, he was god-father to both of them. "Morning uncle Steve" they both said.

"You guys go sit, and I'll make you a special breakfast"

The kids ran over to my table (they knew it well), and took their seats.

"Special breakfast?" I asked.

"Well, you know, sausage and egg baps. They love em!"

"You spoil them mate" I said with a smile

"Morning fuckface, gimme a hug"

We hugged and he asked "how you been?"

"I've been ok mate. Actually really well in fact."

"That's good mate. Really is. Go sit and I'll bring food"

I joined the kids, whilst Chrissy was stood chatting to Willow, who was showing her how to work the coffee machine.

"Here you go my precious angels" Steve said, bringing the baps over a few minutes later. "Get your chops around those"

The kids eyes widened, and they got stuck in. It was always good to see the kids eating. *Hey, you covered that already Jacko.* Yeah I know, but worth repeating.

I enjoyed my cappuccino, as made by Willow's glamorous assistant.

"Was it ok?" she asked, unsure

"It was pretty good actually" I wasn't lying, it really was. Not as good as Willows, but good for a first go.

"You guys want to go see nan and grandad?" I asked

"And Chico!" Elsie boomed

"Yes, and Chico"

I went over and thanked Willow and Steve for the lovely breakfast. I got my card out to pay, to protests form Steve. "You fucking kidding me? I'm treating my gang" he insisted.

"You sure?"

"Get the fuck out you moron"

"Ok mate, thanks"

Took about ten minutes to say our goodbyes, and for Steve to finally let the kids go. Eventually, however, we made our way to the parents' house. And Chico, of course.

Despite the short walk to my parents' house, we got pretty wet; it had started raining whilst we were sat in the cafe. Dad opened the door to four drowned rats, and said as much

"Wow, what a nice surprise! You look like drowned

rats, come on, get inside in the warm" he ushered us in.

"Thanks dad" I said "It's raining pretty bad out there now"

"Well, get your coats off and go get yourselves warm, the fire is on."

We did as told, and were soon huddled around the fire, warming ourselves. Mum appeared from the kitchen, followed by "Chico!" both kids shouted.

"Well now, looks like I've been usurped by the dog!" dad said.

"Looks like it" I agreed. "I'm sure they'll come over and stroke your head in a moment though" I said, mocking

"Funny. Nice to see you haven't lost your sense of humour. If that's what you call it" dad responded.

The kids were fussing over the dog, so mum came over and hugged each of us in turn. "My, you're soaking" she said "Cup of tea?"

"Yeas please" Chrissy said enthusiastically, and followed mum off into the kitchen.

"They seem to be getting on ok" I said to dad, absent mindedly

"We're really happy for you son. It's good to see you happy again"

"Thanks dad, it's a slow process, but I'm getting there. With her help" Felt strange saying this to my dad, as I'd never really talked about the divorce with him. I just assumed that mum would have filtered down our chat to him. Maybe that was wrong of me. "Hey, you fancy a pint sometime?" I asked him

"Sure," he said "That would be nice. It's been a while since I've been to the pub. Not your mother's scene, you know?"

"Yeah, I know. Well, we'll do it one evening this week. How about Tuesday?"

"Sounds good to me" he replied. "We'd better go see what's going on in the kitchen"

I checked on the kids quickly; they were all over Chico, then followed dad.

Mum was in full flow when I walked in, giving Chrissy the full rundown on the family. "And then there's Deirdre in Peterborough, she's a right one. Went right off the rails when her Gerald died, cruises every year. Lord alone knows what she gets up to!" she laughed. Chrissy was fully engaged, and laughed with her.

"Looks like I came in just in time" I said "Poor aunty Deirdre, she's just having fun mum" Gerald had been quite controlling of her, and she was finally free to do all the things she wanted to. Good for her.

"I know" mum said, then turning back to Chrissy "Bless her soul, she's a kind heart" The both laughed.

"Was hoping to find a cup of tea…?" I sort of asked

"Ach you, those days are over. Make your own" mum said, obviously too busy gossiping.

"Ok Deirdre" I said, winking at Chrissy

"Hey!" tea towel came flying across the kitchen.

"Well," I said, picking it up "At least it's not a punch

to the shoulder"

"Can be arranged" Chrissy said, winking at mum.

"You two" I said pointing at each of them in turn "are dangerous together"

I boiled the kettle again, and made tea for myself and dad. We left the ladies to carry on gossiping, and went to see what the kids were up to.

"Hey you guys, Chico surviving?"

"Yes daddy, don't be silly" Elsie said.

I exchanged bemused looks with dad "You're a funny little sausage" he said "Where's my hug anyway? Dog more important now?"

"No grandad" she said, got up, and gave dad a big hug

"Oh there she is, my little nugget" he said hugging her lovingly.

We spent another hour or so at mum and dads, before leaving them to it. We promised to meet up with them later on to walk Chico.

The walk home was both cold and wet, but our spirits were up. Four happy Beckett's walking through the village in the rain, faces beaming with happiness.

Wait. Did you just say four Beckett's? Slow down there Jackie boy, getting ahead of yourself aren't you? Yeah, maybe, but it just felt right saying it. It would take a few years, but we would eventually be four Beckett's. Yeah, eventually. But right now, keep your head out of the clouds. Concentrate. EH? On what? I walked straight into a bollard. *That, dick.*

"Ouch!"

"Hey, you ok there?" Chrissy asked? The kids were both too buy laughing to ask if I was ok, and just kept on walking. "Yeah, just took a bollard straight to the nuts" I said to Chrissy. The slow, sickly pain was starting to make itself known. It's a feeling like no other. Guys, you know what I mean. Ladies, surely not "as bad as childbirth".... Yawn, nothing ever is...wink.

"You're a nutjob" she said, my head eventually back in the game

"Nutjob? You spend too much time around Steve" I said

"He's funny, and quite charming really" she replied, teasing

"Whatever" I shook my head "Let's just get home before I end up in hospital."

"Don't worry, I'll help you" she said, holding my hand. Didn't even register that she was taking the piss; the warmth of her hand in mine made everything else fade into the background.

The kids got home before us, had ditched their wet coats on the floor, and disappeared up to their lairs. "Hey you guys! Thanks for leaving the wet coats on the floor!" I shouted up at them. To my surprise, James came down and picked them up "Sorry dad, I'll hang them out in the utility room"

I gave Chrissy a quizzical look "What is going on with that boy?" she just flashed a smile in response. "Ah, I get it" I said, and rolled my eyes. Jesus.

With no real plans for the rest of the day, other than the dog walk later on, we just spent the day doing random stuff around the house. I put a load of washing on, Chrissy went off with polish and a cloth to do the dusting. The kids were in their rooms; James no doubt on the PlayStation, and Elsie likely chatting away to her friends whilst watching whatever movie they were all into at the moment. It was all pretty normal. We'd settled into routine. *Hey, that's what families do right?* Yes, it is. We're a family. And that was a comforting thought. Hey, inner voice... *Yes?* Thank you for being on my side. *Welcome, can't promise it's going to last forever though eh.* Well, I'll just make the most of it for now then. Thanks.

"Earth to Jack?"

"What?"

"Where the hell were you? Miles away"

"Oh, you know, just...you know."

"Ok... You want a drink?"

"Oh, erm, yes please."

"Of...?"

"Tea?" I asked, hesitatingly.

"Tea will do" she said and went off to the kitchen.

Wow, I need to work on making my inner voice conversations less noticeable. *Yeah you do fuckwad, she's going to think you're a nutter.* Yeah, constructive, thanks for that. *Always here to help.*

"Here you go" Chrissy said, returning a few minutes later with two mugs of tea.

"Mmm, thanks"

"So, what you want to do for dinner tonight?" she asked, sipping her tea.

"Hadn't really thought about it to be honest" I said.

"You want me to do something?" she asked

"Sure, if you want to"

"You know I do" she said. "So, tell me what the kids like and dislike"

"Right…" she said after I'd finished reeling off the list of love and hate. "How about tagliatelle with salmon, broccoli, and peas in a creamy sauce?"

"You seem to have caught on that we love Italian food" I said chuckling "That sounds perfect. We'd need to go to the shop though"

"Well, kind of fits in with my own tastes" she said

"Let me get my g=bag and we'll take a drive"

"Guys! We're just off to the shop, won't be long I have my phone"

"Ok dad!" form James. That was enough.

We drove over to Sainsbury's in Ramsey, and walked around in perfect happiness.

We got all the fresh ingredients she needed to cook up a feast, then stood for a while in the beer aisle, choosing a few different ales each. Chrissy liked the darker beers, which suited me.

"Hi Jack"

What? I turned to see who it was, but knew already. Fuck. Fucking fuck.

"Oh, hi Helen" Shit. Shitty shit McShitty fuck. This was going to be awkward.

I blushed, and didn't know what to do, just hoping

the floor would open up and swallow me whole.

She was stood there, looking at me. She knew how fucked up this was, and was enjoying seeing me squirm. Chrissy however, was having none of it.

"Hi, Helen is it? I'm Chrissy" she stuck out a hand. Oh, dear God no. What are you doing???

Jackie boy, this is fucked up! Yeah, tell me something I don't know.

Helen stared for a split second, not knowing what to do. It was only a split second, but it was enough. Well played my love, well played.

"Hi, nice to meet you" she said awkwardly, shaking hands ever so briefly.

She shook it off, and turned back to me "didn't expect to see you here Jack" she said.

"Just shopping" I said

She looked down into our trolley and noted "Beer shopping it seems?" Judgemental. Like alcohol isn't allowed; it makes you a bad parent. Chrissy came to the rescue again. "Actually, we're food shopping for dinner tonight. I'm doing the kids fresh pasta. There are four bottles of beer in the trolley, which is pretty below average for two people for a week"

"Ah, I see" Helen seemed uneasy. Not used to being countered. "You live together?"

I froze. Fuck.

"No," Chrissy said "I'm just staying over for the weekend so we can have some fun with the kids"

She keeps mentioning the kids Jack! She's doing it on purpose! Helen's going to blow! Shit. She was. She was making a real point of it too.

"Staying over?" Helen responded, looking at me?

"Yes, staying over" Chrissy said, keeping the focus firmly on her, not me. "Oh, don't worry though, I'm sleeping in the office on a put up bed. Hope that's ok with you?" she added sarcastically.

Helen didn't quite know what to do with herself. She looked steadfastly at me, not wanting to acknowledge Chrissy's presence.

"Well, I guess it's none of my business" she said "I'm just thinking of the kids"

"You're right" Chrissy said "It is none of your business. Even if we were sharing a bed, it would be none of your business. Come on Jack"

We walked off, leaving Helen stupefied, and fuming inside. I could see it in her eyes.

"What the fuck was that?" I asked as we turned a corner.

"Jack, she's trying to dominate you, even now. She needed to be put in her place."

Oh shit, now she was angry too. I had a knack for making women angry with me. Sigh.

She looked around, to make sure Helen was gone, then hugged me "That was terrifying" she confessed "I've never felt so awkward in my life"

"You wouldn't think it" I Said "You handled that like a pro. Far better than I did."

"She wanted to belittle you, question your parenting, and our relationship. Not on my watch" she said defiantly.

"Hey..." I said

"What?"

I kissed her "I love you"

"I love you too. Let's get out of here and never come back"

"That's probably exactly what she's thinking. Come on"

We made for the till, and casually walked to the car. Running would have been quicker, but we didn't want to show that we'd been rattled by Helen.

We drove home in silence. Not because we were angry, I guess we were just lost in our own thoughts.

When we pulled into the drive, Chrissy said "We need to find somewhere new to shop, that was uncomfortable"

"Yeah" I agreed "Maybe the other Sainsbury's in March would be better"

"Are you ok?" she asked

"Yeah. That was weird though. I didn't know she had it in her to be that nasty"

"She's threatened by me I guess. Just angry that you are with someone. She doesn't like that you have moved on"

"I guess that's true" I agreed. It made sense. I wouldn't want to see her with someone else, so why should she? "We'll do our best to avoid her from now on"

"Agreed."

"Before you say something to really piss her off" I added

Punch to shoulder? Yeah, why not. "Ouch!"
"Dick. Come on, let's get inside"

Sidebar?

Have you ever had an uncomfortable run in with your ex? Met her unexpectedly in a supermarket or somewhere? Its shit right. If I was on my own, it wouldn't have been so bad, but she saw me with Chrissy, which was bad. Fortunately, she witnessed first-hand how confident Chrissy is, and highly protective of me and our relationship. She was defending her man. *What, because you couldn't?* Yeah, I couldn't. We've been through this; I'm not the most confident person in the world.

Anyways, we went in and Chrissy went off and started dinner. I went up to check on the kids, and to give them the chocolate we had just bought for them. Obviously under the strict conditions that it be consumed after dinner. Not sure I really needed to say it, because they were both really looking forward to dinner. I know this made Chrissy happy, she was desperate to be pseudo mother to the kids.

I went up to the office, and fired up a laptop. Wow, quite a few videos to do next week, with a couple of long ones from my new client; factory tours. This was going to be a busy week.

I went back to see how Chrissy was getting on; just perfect thanks, but could do with a glass of wine. I obliged, and poured one for myself too.

"Right, that's gotto simmer for an hour or so. You

want to call your mum and see if they want to go out now?"

I called mum, and arranged to meet at the bridge in 5. "Kids! We're going out to walk Chico!" I called upstairs. Literally a minute later, the kids had coats on and were ready to go.

"Wow, impressive" I remarked.

Mum and dad were there when we walked up, and we all went off, Chico leading the way.

It was a great walk; the parents looked happy, and I hadn't seen them out so much in ages. Chico really was good for them. We got home about 40 minutes later, and sent the kids off to wash their hands. I set the table, and it was time to eat. I was a bit nervous about whether they would actually eat the pasta. Can't remember them ever having had salmon before. I needn't have worried; they devoured it. And both had seconds. Wow.

After dinner, James volunteered to do the dishes (what the very....?), so Chrissy and I went and sat in the living room with a glass of wine. This was another perfect day, except for the shopping shiteness. We'd seen the people we loved, again, apart from the shopping shiteness, and the kids had walked Chico. It was all good. I kissed Chrissy.

"What was that for?" she asked.

"For being my knight in shining armour" I said "Here's to you; cheers my Lady" we clinked glasses and had a giggle about the whole affair.

The kids had ice cream for dessert, and stalked off upstairs, not to be seen again until morning.

"So, what did you want to do tonight?" I asked.
"Mr Beckett! Really!" she did that whole Victorian maiden thing again.
"Am I allowed to punch your shoulder?" I asked
"No sir, you are not; that's my thing"
"Ah, maybe I'll just…..tickle then!" I lunged at her and tickled her mercilessly. It was hilarious.
"Stop it!" she managed between laughing fits. "I need a wee!"
I stopped "Oh, sorry"
"You're so easy Beckett" Naturally, I resumed my tickle torture.
We settled down, and watched a bit of telly. There wasn't much on, never is. Chrissy suggested a new series Swiss she'd heard about, so we watched it. It was in Swiss (German), with subtitles, but was awesome. If you're interested, its called The Undertaker (Der Bestatter); it's ace.

Bedtime eventually came. Yes! I'd literally been waiting for it since we got up. I get to lay next to this beautiful woman. My God, I'm so lucky. Now I know I said that in my head, so she must be a mind reader, because "I can hear what you're thinking Beckett"
"What?"
"You. I know you've been waiting for this all day you saddo"
"There's nothing sad about sleeping with you" I countered
"Come on then you sad case. No funny business

though"
"Promise" I said.
After teeth and her beauty regime, we lay there in each other's arms, just enjoying the moment.
"Love you Beckett"
"Love you Lenoir"
Sounds like a scene from the Walton's, but I didn't care. I wanted her to know I loved her, as much as she wanted me to know that she loved me. I fell asleep, the sweet smell of her perfume filling my unconscious mind, setting me adrift in a sea of pleasant dreams.

Bon soir Mr Holmes.

DAY 15

Sunday, 31st of March.

I woke, and turned to hug my beautiful woman. Oh, she's not there. Hmm. Ok, where is she? I got up, and went down to see where she was.
"Morning stud" she said
"Wha...?" confused. *She's kidding dickhead.* Ah, ok.
She winked "Coffee there, go for it"
I drank generously from the hot coffee, it was needed.
"Hope you don't mind, I woke and thought I'd do pancakes" She stopped. "They like pancakes right? I mean, what kid doesn't?"
"Erm, mine?" I said.
"What? Shit. You're joking" she sort of asked
"Yeah, they love pancakes"
No punch to shoulder, but I'm sure I'd just banked one for later...
"You know it's only just gone half seven right?" I asked
"Yeah, I'll just keep them warm in the oven till they get up"
"Ok. That mean I have time for a shower?" I asked,

finishing my coffee.
"I would say so. Need a hand?"
"Wha....?" *She's doing it again dickhead.* Ah, ok.
"Funny. You're funny" I said and went off to shower as she just giggled.
As I was getting dressed, something made me think about Steve; he'd asked if Chrissy could have a look at his books. Shit. I'd completely forgotten. I went down, and asked her straight away. "Sure, I'll pop over in the morning. I don't have anything work wise till one o'clock"
"Thank you, lifesaver. I completely forgot"
"I'm sure it'll be fine, I mean, how bad can it be right?"
"This is Steve we're talking about" I reminded her.
"But he's usually pretty good with it. I think it's just the employee thing he's worried about"
"I'll check it tomorrow. You want more coffee?"
"Sure" I text Steve and let him know

Him: I knew you'd forget you penis.
Me: Sorry mate, but sorted now
Him: Cool, hopefully it'll be ok
Me: Sure it will.

I'd deserved that. I knew this was important to him, but with everything else that had happened, I'd just forgotten.
"What did he say?" she asked from behind me
"He called me a penis"
"You deserved that" she said
"Yeah, I know."

Sounds coming from upstairs indicated imminent child appearances.

"Oh shit, I forgot to set the table" she said "Quick!"

We quickly set the table, and I was just pouring the orange juice when Elsie appeared

"Morning beautiful" I said, kissing her head. "Here, have some juice"

"Morning daddy, morning Chrissy" she said and sat at the table

James joined a minute later "What's for breakfast?"

"I made pancakes" Chrissy said

Chants of excitement from both. Chrissy brought the stack of pancakes from the oven, and we got stuck in.

A blissful family breakfast. Never grows old.

After, Chrissy and I sat with a coffee whilst the kids did the dishes.

"You ready for tomorrow?" I asked

"Tomorrow?"

"The house, you said it'll be transferred tomorrow"

"Ah, well, I'm not sure it actually goes that quickly. I can start decorating though. They said the house would be emptied out on Saturday, and they'd be leaving on Monday morning. I'm meeting them there to get the keys before they go"

"Ah, that makes sense. Thought about what you're going to do with the place?"

"Not really, don't see why we would keep it, so probably sell it."

I thought about it for a second. She had a point; what purpose would it serve? I had a home, and she seemed happy to be here, so what was she going to do with it? Rent it out? To whom? I'm sure there's a market, but being a landlady? That's hard work. Or....

"Hey, just a thought" I said
"Hmmm?"
"What about a holiday let?"
"Like an airbnb?" she asked.
"Yeah. We could do it up, and rent it out in the summer. You'd only have to make enough to cover the council tax, bills, and maintenance. Not like you need to turn a massive profit"
"Hmm, yeah, maybe. I don't know Jack. I'll have a think."
"Ok, just floating ideas" I said.
"I could rent it out I suppose" she said suddenly "I do know someone looking for a place"
"Oh, cool. Who?"
"Your ex-wife?" she said
"Holy shit" I said, and went to punch her shoulder
"No! No!" she laughed "I was only kidding you dick"
"Not funny Lenoir" I said, trying to keep a straight face.
"In the meantime, what are we going to do today?" I asked, changing the subject.
"Not sure, what do you usually do?"
"We usually go somewhere for a walk, just to get the kids out. After, I just tend to potter around, and

the kids do their own thing." I explained

"You want to go for a walk?" she asked, looking out of the window.

It was pouring down. Shit. "Erm, not really"

"No, I didn't think so. What else can we do?" she asked.

"Welcome to parenting 101. Fortunately, the kids are of an age where they can entertain themselves, so we don't really need to do much. I'll speak to them, and see what's going on"

"Is this what it's always like?"

"What?"

"Parenting, feels like a lot of pressure to keep the family entertained"

"It does?" I must have looked very confused and worried.

"Don't get me wrong, I'm not complaining, I just mean, you know…." She trailed off, losing her train of thought.

"Hey, I get it." I said "Parenting is hard work, but the hardest years are done now. It is a lot of work, you have to have several ideas in mind for things to do, depending on the weather. I have a go-to list of places. May get a bit repetitive, but they don't really mind too much. Neither do I; it's about being out and about. Make sense?" It barely made sense to me, let alone anyone else!

"Yes, of course. Guess it'll take some time for me to put together my own list"

"Yep, after that, it's easy. You just rattle off a list of possibilities, and they'll choose one. Or,

sometimes they're happy to just stay home."
"They do?"
"Yeah, sometimes they have homework, sometimes James just likes to game with his mates, and sometimes Elsie just wants to stay in and watch stuff"

Tangent.
As a parent, does that make sense? To me it does. I always want to get my kids out for a couple of hours, then I'm pretty happy they do what they want. I do have a list of places to go, and I do rattle them off till one sticks. We have our favourite, and that's what usually gets chosen. Repetition doesn't matter to me, its being outside that matters. Getting harder these days; kids social lives is online a lot, and they don't play out like we used to. As a Gen X, I'm likely the last generation to have that in childhood. We used to be out all day, and just come home for food. The next generations don't have that, and it will slowly die out. We worry about it, because we want our kids to be active, like we were. After us, nobody will care because they never experienced it. Sad really. But anyway, old man rant over…

I walked to the stairs and shouted up "Guys, you want to do anything today?"
James responded "no", and Elsie actually came down and asked if we could go see Uncle Steve later.
After she had gone back upstairs, I turned to

Chrissy and said "See? Easy" Wink.

"I guess I'll just do a bit of reading or something then" she responded, shrugging her shoulders.

"We'll potter about, and go to the caff for lunch?" I asked, sort of

"Yep, sounds good"

And so, the normality, call it monotony, of family life sets in. You just have a routine. I went off and cleaned the bathroom, and Chrissy sat in the window reading a book (portrait of Dorian Grey).

Another tangent? Oh, go on then... (or follow on...)

Yeah, the normality of family life. It's not always excitement and fun; sometimes it's just sitting around doing your own thing. Parents can catch up on cleaning/housework, the kids on whatever they do. It's quiet, not a lot of interaction. We just plod on. And, it's amazing how quickly the day can pass by. Before you know it, most of the day has gone. And you know what? Sometimes, that's ok. The kids don't need to be out and about all the time, they are sometimes just happy to do their own thing. And, let's face it, as parents, we don't always have enough time to do the basics like housework, diy, etc. Or, let's face it, stuff for yourself. Your hobbies and interests. How often do you get to do that? Think about it. It's so important to have "me" time. You need time off to do the things you enjoy. You're still parenting, but just not actively. Hope that all kind of made sense?

Parenting isn't always about taking your kids out and having fun. There will be quiet days. And that's ok. I could fill a book on parenting alone, but that's not the subject of this book.

I finished the bathroom, and found Chrissy asleep in the window seat, book in hand. She looked peaceful, so I left her and went to get myself a drink. It was only just after ten, so I went up to the office to get ahead on work. A while later, Chrissy came up to find me.
"You're working?" she asked
"Oh hey, yeah. You were asleep, and the kids were still doing their thing, so I came up here." I saved my progress, and shut down. "There, done. Time is it?"
"Let me just check on my flashy new watch" she said theatrically "Oh, its five to twelve. Hey, that's lunch time" she knew this already of course, she was making a point.
"Point taken. Let's round up the crew and make a move."
"They're already downstairs, waiting" she winked.
"Ah, I see. Sounds like a conspiracy…"
We went down, and there they were, waiting.
"Daddy, I'm hungry. Can we go now please?" Elsie said. James nodded his agreement.
"Yes, I get it. I get it. Come on then"
I grabbed the keys and herded them out to the car. We drove the short distance, and parked at the back of the café. It wasn't hoofing it down

anymore, but still that fine drizzle that gets you equally as soaked.
Tinkle.

Mini tangent. If I may, before proceeding.
As the writer of this award winning work of semi-fiction, I *love* it when the "tinkle" bit comes. It heralds excitement. Steve is such a great character, he swears, he's fun, and he brightens up the book. My opinion, but I love him. In reality, I love him too, as he's a great guy, and my oldest friend. Doesn't swear as much in reality, I just exaggerated it...
Though I don't see him very much anymore, he's always there. Always first to ask how I am if something is wrong. I call him Sven though (goes back to our Uni days, I think year 1, sat towards the back on the wooden benches in Analogue Electronics? That lecturer we ended up giving a nervous breakdown?). Love you bud.
Just had to say that.

Anyhoo, back to semi-reality...

Tinkle.

No quippy remark from Steve as we walked in, he was busy serving two older ladies.
"You sit yourselves down girls and I'll bring it right over" they giggled and made some comment about not having been girls for quite a few years, and went to their table. There were a few others in, but it wasn't busy. He looked up. Our turn for

commentary. Stand by…

"Well, well, look what the cat dragged in. If it isn't the Becketts". Ta-da! Shock. No swearing; he doesn't swear in front of the kids. "To what do we owe the pleasure?"

"Moring Stephen" Chrissy said, and kissed him on the cheek.

"Eh! Steady on girl!" Love it. She can shock him as much as he can her. Good girl.

"Come 'ere you two" he said to the kids, and they ran around the counter to give hugs.

Even though the kids were getting a bit older, they still loved hugging their uncle Steve. He used to be able to lift them both at the same time, but those days have long gone. "My lovely monsters! Go sit and choose what you want, anything, your dad's paying!"

I just gave him a knowing look, as if to say "Fuck you, I was going to anyway"

The kids ran off, menus in hand and sat at our table.

"Morning sunshine"

"Sunshine?" I said, confused

"What? No fuckface today Stephen?" Chrissy asked, making herself laugh.

He rolled his eyes "Ok, ok. Morning arse nuggets" he looked at us in turn "Better?"

Chrissy was giggling like mad. I just said "Better. You had me worried"

"Here's me trying to better myself, and you two muppets drag me back down to gutter level"

"Swearing suits you, it's what makes you, you" Chrissy said

"So, I'm basically just here for your amusement?" he asked, trying his best to look serious.

"Basically, yes" I said

"Fuck you, nutsack. Go sit"

More giggling from Chrissy. "Not you girl, you get to stay here, I need a word. In my office" he said, to her.

"Ooh, I feel like a naughty school girl again!" She said

Steve and I instantly looked at each other; him with a bemused look, me just rolling my eyes. Smooth fucker.

"Oh, actually, before you fuck off, you'll have to make your own drinks. Willow is off today, and I'm in a business meeting". They went off to talk finance in the office (kitchen).

"What the fuck ever." I said, and walked around the counter to get the kids' drinks.

Chrissy joined us a few minutes later "You look happy" I said, perhaps too loudly as it merited a comment from Steve "I aim to please"

Whatever. "You had a good chat?"

"Yes, it was actually. He's in a pretty good place with his finances, I have a few ideas to go through with him tomorrow. You were right, he is very worried"

"Yeah, it's been on his mind a lot, and he's terrified he's doing something wrong. Thank you for helping" I said

"Hey, that's what I'm here for isn't it? Besides, I get free barista training from Willow out of it"

"Noice. Sounds like a good deal"

"Yep, I'm keen to learn so I can help out if required. I want to be part of the team, you know?"

"You *are* part of the team. Maybe the most useless part, but still…" didn't get to finish, punch landed on shoulder before I could. "Ouch!"

"You deserved that daddy" Elsie said.

"What? You as well?" I lamented "Is *anyone* still on my side??"

Shaking heads all round. "Nice….nice. Thanks"

"Who's paying for this lunch again?" I asked, mockingly.

"I will if it makes it better" Chrissy said.

"No argument here" I said, holding up my hands.

"Right, let's order" she said and stuck her hand up "Waiter, we're ready to order"

Steve came over, muttering under his breath.

"What can I get for you lovely people" he said, his hands around my neck

Laughter all round. Followed by orders shouted out at random.

"Hey whoa! Slow down!" he moaned

Orders received, he retreated to the kitchen to get to work.

Chrissy turned to me and asked "You want a coffee? I'll make it"

"How could I possibly refuse? Latte please"

"Ok!" she said excitedly, and trotted off to the java

machine.
I chatted with the kids whilst she did that, and Steve prepped our food.
It was another picture perfect happy family occasion, and I loved every second of it.

After devouring our lunch, we helped Steve tidy, and said our goodbyes. He hugged the kids tightly, and even Chrissy got a hug. "See you later mate" I said when it was my turn
"Yeah, good to see you mate, thanks. And you hold on to that one, she's a peach"
"I will"
We walked back to the car, in the slightly heavier rain, and drove home. Happy Becketts.

Side notey:
So you'll notice that as a family group, we're being referred to as the Becketts. It felt good. Even though we weren't married, people had accepted Chrissy as part of the family. It was good to hear, and made her feel like she belonged. We would of course be "The Becketts" in the future, but we didn't know that yet. Or we did, but kept it to ourselves as hope.

Back in the room...

Only a few hours till the kids went home. Ok Jack, take a breath and hold it together.
I hated Sunday. It meant I had to let my kids go. I'd spend the next 5 mornings waking up to a quiet, empty house. I want them to stay. They

belong here, in their home. *Hey, dickhead, you forget something. What? That tasty bird you trapped will be here all week.* Of course. Yes, thank you. Oh, just one thing? *Yes?* You will refer to her as Chrissy thanks, nothing demeaning or nasty. Got It?
Fair enough. Soz.
I was on a collision course with the hard deck, and owed inner voice one. *Yeah you do!* But... *Oh.* But, then it insulted her, so it can fucking do one. *Dammit. Ok.* Narrow avoidance of a depressive funk. Good. Focus on the positive; you had a great weekend, and they're in school most of the weekdays anyway right? True. Balances Jack, balances.

"Hey, You good?" Chrissy shook me from my daydream.
"Yeah, I'm good. I'm good" I said.
"Good. I'm going to teach Elsie how to do her nails, is that ok?"
"Yeah sure, of course" I said
"Cool. Just checking. Didn't know if you thought she was too young maybe"
"Nah, it good" I said. I would regret it tomorrow, but that's in the future. You can probably guess why. *Hey, this to do with Helen?* What? Nobody asked you. *Oh ok. I miss her, she had a fantastic pair of...*" Enough! Fuck off! Remember whose side you're supposed to be on?? *Yeah, soz. My bad...*
Dammit. Why is my inner voice such a dick?? *Because I'm you?* No, you're not. You're the opposite

of me, that's why you're here. To fill my head full of shite. *Erm, not being funny Jackie boy, but I've had a good look around here, and it IS full of shite.* I swear to God I'll get some tablets from a head doctor to shut you up. *Speaking of which. Tomorrow?* I had the appointment with that woman! Shit. I'd forgotten. *Lol.*

James was upstairs on the phone, so I was on my own for a bit. I decided to watch a bit of tv to kill the time. And that time came all too soon. James came and sat next to me, after putting his bag down. It was too soon surely?? I looked at my watch, and saw that it wasn't; it was four o'clock.

"Hey buddy, you ok?" I asked him

"Yeah, you know. I just don't like saying bye dad. You know?"

Instant sadness. "I know mate, I'm really sorry."

"Not your fault dad, but the situation sucks right?"

"You have no idea how hard it is to watch you guys leave" I said "I hate it. But, we have to be strong and get through this. Ok?"

"Yeah, ok. Still sucks though" he said, sighing.

I made a mental reminder to take the time to talk to the kids individually about what was going on. Can' be easy on them either.

Elsie and Chrissy joined us, and showed off their beautifully painted nails. "Ooh, very nice" I said.

Elsie beamed with pride. "Good work Ello, really good"

"Thank you daddy"

"Have you packed your bag? It's time to go" I said.

Her happy mood instantly disappeared, but she tried not to let it show. "Yes, I have it upstairs" she said and ran off. Chrissy and I exchanged looks of sympathy. "Poor thing" she said.

Yeah, I thought, poor thing. Despite that, I felt incredibly proud Ello; she was obviously upset, but trying ever so hard not to let it show in case it upset me. Breathe Jack! Keep it together now!

Elsie came back, holding her bag "Ready daddy"

I kissed her head "Ok Ello, let's go"

We all got in the car, and drove over to Ramsey to drop the kids at me ex in-laws. Needless to say, it was a difficult goodbye, and I cried. Not till they had gone inside though. Chrissy held me "Hey, it's going to be ok. The week will fly by and they'll be with us again"

"I know, it's just so hard, you know?" Still crying.

"I know baby, I know. Come on, let's get you home"

We got back in the car and drove home.

The rest of the evening was pretty glum; I was quiet, despite Chrissy's best efforts. She understood though. We watched a movie, bought more stuff online, and looked at where she wanted to go in Florence. I booked it, which made her happy. I was happy on the inside, but the struggle to show it was immense. I think I managed, but she probably knew it wasn't real.

We eventually went up to bed, and I started crying uncontrollably as soon as the lights went out. I had crashed. Hard. Chrissy did her best to comfort me,

but the level of grief was just too great.
I eventually fell asleep in her arms; my head was exhausted.

Fuck you Helen.

Bitch.

DAY 16

Monday, 1st of April.

The alarm woke me with a start. I silenced it and sat up. Chrissy was still asleep, she didn't need to be up early. I sat back and took a moment. April fool's day. Fuck sake. I really hoped today wouldn't be a disaster. I was sick to death of being a burden to my love, I was sure she probably felt the same. Didn't she? Please don't. Nah, she's ok, she loves you. For some reason. I know you're a dick, inner voice, but thanks for the veiled words of encouragement. What the fuck does that mean? Welcome I guess. Quietly, I go out of bed, and went off to make some tea. I didn't make one for Chrissy, as I thought she'd probably prefer a lay in after looking after my pathetic self last night. Shrug it off Jack, don't let the negativity dominate your day. I won't. I'm on it. I finished my tea, and put my running gear on. Treadmill today I think. I did a 5k, and went off to shower. The shower was soothing, therapeutic. I ran it cold for a few secs at the end, and emerged completely awake and ready for the day. Chrissy was still asleep. Couldn't blame her. I took some clothes and dressed in the office. Went down and made some toast and a coffee. I was just about to go up to the office to start work when I heard noise upstairs. I went up, and gave her the breakfast. "I made you breakfast" I said. You lying bastard! Shush! I need a win here. Ok, I'll let you have this one.

"Oh, that's really nice of you, thanks" she said, gratefully accepting.

"I'm sorry about last night. I don't know what happened."

"Hey, I've told you before; you don't need to apologise for being human."

"I know, but I just feel like I'm constantly letting you down"

"You're not. You've been through a lot Jack. Hell, you're still going through a lot. It makes you human, not weak" She kissed me "I love you for it"

"Thanks, still feel a bit bad though. I have the appointment with that woman today"

"Yep, quarter past twelve. Don't be late, you need this"

"Hmmm, part of me was hoping you were going to say it was an April fool's day stunt"

"That's funny" she laughed "I didn't even realise that was today"

"Yeah, all day sadly."

"You'll be fine Jack, it's just an initial chat. Just to get to know each other"

"I know. And I'm sure it'll be good. I need it to be."

"I'm sure it will" she leaned over and kissed my forehead.

"Right, I'll leave you to wake up, I have a tonne of

work to get through this week"
"Ok, and thank you again, it was lovely of you" she said, holding up her coffee cup
"Welcome" I kissed her and went off to work.

I was lost in a world of my own, working hard, when she kissed me on the cheek "Jesus!"
"Hi" smile "Sorry I disturbed you mid flow, but I'm off to talk to Steve about his finances"
"Ah yeah, ok, hope you get it sorted out"
"I will, not much to sort really. Hey, don't forget your appointment right?"
"I won't" I said, "Look, I've set an alarm" I showed her my phone with the alarm set for 11.30.
"Ok, hope it goes well" she kissed me and left.

When the alarm went off, I was almost finished with

my 3rd video of the morning. I was making good progress. I saved and got ready to leave. The drive shouldn't take long, Chatteris isn't that far away. I wanted to leave enough time to find the place, and somewhere to park, so I grabbed my coat and got in the car. *Deep breath Jack. You got this.* Yeah, I do. *Let's go then.* Ok. *So go.* Ok. *No, not ok. Start the car and leave.* I will. *When? Time is ticking.* Fuck, ok. I started the car and made my way to Chatteris.
It was only a 15 minute drive to Chatteris, traffic was light. I found the place easy enough. In the day of google maps, everything is easy to find right. There was parking outside, so I pulled into a space. Looked at watch. 5 minutes to go. *Be strong.* I will.

You'll be fine. Will I? What if she thinks I'm insane? *Well, you do have conversations with your inner voice....* Fuck, shit, balls. OK, I'm going in. I got out and walked up to the door. Breathe... I rang the bell, and almost instantly it was opened.
"Hi, you must be Jack"
"Erm, yes, I am"
"Hi Jack, I'm Pam, please, come in."
I followed her in, and she led me to a room that had been converted into a therapy room; comfy sofas, soft lighting, neutral colours. Everything you would imagine it to be.
"Please, sit" she said
"Oh, erm, thank you." I sat on the sofa, opposite her chair. She sat and picked up a notepad and pen.
"So, Jack. You're probably a bit nervous, and wondering how this is going to work. Well, first off; don't be nervous. I am not here to make you nervous, I am here, hopefully, to help."
"Thank you" I said "I am a bit nervous, but I think only because I'm not sure what to expect, and talking to a stranger about my feelings is a bit odd"
She laughed "Perfectly understandable. We're just going to talk, no hocus pocus, just chatting. I'll lead the conversation with some questions, but I'll be mostly listening and making notes. Does that sound ok?"
"Yes, it does" I said "Apologies for being so nervous"
"No need to be Jack, I get it. Before we start, can I pour you some tea? I just made a pot" she nodded

towards the tea set on the table in front of me.
"Yes, please. That would be nice"
"Perfect. How do you take it?"
"Just milk please, no sugar"
"Hmm, interesting..." she said, and poured my tea.
"Oh?" I asked, voice tinged with worry.
She winked "A little joke Jack, just to break the ice"
I laughed. "Thank you, its working"
"Good" she smiled. "Now, why don't you start us off by telling me why you think you're here."
"Ok, where do I begin?" I said
"Wherever you want. I'm just going to listen"
"Well, I guess I should start by telling you about the last year or so of my life..." I started.
I talked for about 30 minutes, only stopped occasionally when she asked a question.
"So, my girlfriend Chrissy suggested I come see you to try get my head better. Does that make sense?"
She sat for a long moment, and said "Sounds like you've had quite a lot of negative experiences Jack. I appreciate you sharing them with me; that must have been difficult. From what you have told me, and please realise I'm making a rush judgement here, I can tell that you suffer quite badly with anxiety, exasperated by difficult experiences. The conversations you have with your inner voice, is you, trying to make yourself better. The fact that it had gone from being a negative voice to a more positive influence, tells me it is working. I can help you Jack. No magic involved, I will simply aid you

in completing your recovery"

"Well, you haven't had me committed, so I guess there's hope" I joked.

She laughed. "There is hope Jack, and I want to help you finish your journey. With your permission and help of course.

"I think that would be acceptable" I said, holding out my hand

She shook it. "Brilliant. Let me type up my notes, and have a think about a wellness plan, and I'll be in touch. Sound ok?"

"Sounds ok" I said with a smile.

"Excellent. See? Nothing to be nervous about right?"

"No, you're right. I feel a bit silly"

"Don't. It was a big step for you to come here Jack. I saw you struggle with yourself to get out of the car. You should be proud"

"Thank you. For everything, I really appreciate your time" I said, rising.

"My pleasure Jack I don't do it for nothing of course" she winked "But it won't cost you the earth"

"I wasn't too worried about the financial side" I confessed "I just want to get better"

"Oh don't say that, my price just doubled" she said

"Eh?"

"Another joke Jack. I have standard fees, all listed on my website." she laughed

"I think we're going to get on just fine Pam" I said

"I'm glad. I'll send you an email, and we'll make

some appointments. Nice meeting you Jack"
She showed me to the door.
"Nice meeting you Pam, I really enjoyed it"
"Good. That's important" she smiled "Take care Jack, see you soon"
"Bye Pam, thanks again" I said, and walked off to the car. I felt great. Fucking great. Mega fucking fuck fuck great. I hadn't felt this relived and calm in months. I drove over to Steve's cafe, hoping to catch Chrissy there so could tell her all about it.

My mood hadn't diminished an iota by the time I walked through the cafe door.
Tinkle
"Fuck me! Again??" Steve called from behind the counter "Oi, Lenoir, your man's here"
Chrissy looked poked her head around the coffee machine "Hey! Gimme a sec, go sit!" she was all excited. She finished making a coffee for a lady sat by the door, and skipped over. "So? How did it go"
I stood, took her in my arms, and kissed her passionately.
"Whoa! Hey, get a fucking room you two!" Steve shouted over, much to the delight of his female customer base.
"Wow! To what do I owe THAT pleasure??" Chrissy asked
"That, was to thank you for setting up this meeting. It was fucking brilliant. I feel so good its unreal"
"Wow, ok, tell me all about it" she said excitedly.

We sat, and I told her everything that had happened. It felt good.
"Oh Jack I'm so happy for you" she said, throwing her arms around me. "I was a bit scared that you wouldn't go"
"Me too, but I'm so glad I did"
"Me too, you seem like a different person, its amazing"
"I feel like a different person" I said "Don't know how long it lasts for, but I'm going to enjoy every second of it while it does"
I wasn't lying; I felt like a completely different person. Probably would wear off in a while, but I didn't care. I had achieved something; the first step in my healing process. I wasn't sure how long it would take, but I was on the path to healing myself. That was all that mattered.

Side note: I still see Pam on and off all these years later. Although better, sometimes I just feel like I could do with a boost.

"We should celebrate" she said "Oi, fuckwad!" she shouted over to Steve.
He stopped and mouthed "What the fuck?" I was sure from their expressions that most of the ladies in the caff were thinking exactly the same
"Me?" Steve said, unsure of what to do
"Yeah you. Beers tonight, bring Willow. Meet you in the George at seven"
Steve was lost for words, and just nodded.
Holy shit, I thought. What a woman.

We left a dumbstruck Steve behind, and drove home. "I'm so proud of you" she said with her head on my shoulder.

"Thank you, I think I'm proud of myself too."

We got home, and went our separate ways. Me to the kitchen with my mobile office, Chrissy to the office to do her meetings and whatever else she does. I didn't care. Work just happened in a haze. I'd finished another 2 videos by tea time, and called it a day. I could hear Chrissy talking upstairs, so left her to it. I showered and changed ready to go out and have some fun with our friends. Our best friends.

Life was good.

Life was fucking great.

Well done Jack. Thanks, inner voice.

Oh, and that Chrissy chick?

Yes? Careful…

What a woman.

Fist bump.

I sat in the kitchen with a beer, catching up on texts from the kids, mum, etc. whilst Chrissy got herself ready upstairs. When she came down, I *had* to stop what I was doing and just stare.

"What you staring at?" she asked, paranoid.

"You" I said

"Something wrong?" she started checking herself over

"No. Nothing is wrong"

"What then?"

"You are just so beautiful" I said with wide eyes. She was. She really was. She was wearing dark jeans with walking boots, a plaid shirt, and her hair tied back but with two small braids running through it.
"Ach, give over" she said, coyly, and blushed. Result.
"Sorry, just speaking my mind"
"Never stop" she said, kissing me. I never have. I always tell her how good she looks, as soppy as that sounds. It's true, and it's important to me that she know I think she's beautiful.
"It's only half past six, you want to go get pint before they get there?" I said
"Yeah, let's go"

We found a table for four in the pub, which wasn't very busy. Chrissy insisted on getting me a beer, so we stood at the bar seeing what was on tap.
"I'll try the Porter" I said
"Yeah, me too. And some crisps" she smiled, and ordered.
We sat, and talked for a bit about the counselling, until I realised something.
"Hey, how did you get on with the house today?"
"Oh" she said, taking a sip of beer "It was great. We had a bit of a chat, and they are happy for me to do whatever I want to and with the house. The transfer will probably take a couple of weeks, but I have the keys"
"That's great" I said "I'm glad it's all gone so well"

"Yeah, me too. It's been a tough time, but a lot of positive has come out of a tragedy"
"Cheers to that, and to Mary"
"Cheers. To Mary" she said, and we clinked glasses.
"It's been a weird couple of weeks hasn't it?" she said
"Yeah, a lot has happened. Hopefully it'll be quieter going forward"
"Let's hope so. A bit of normality would be bliss to be honest"
"Normality may be boring, but it's comforting" I agreed
A minute or so later, Steve and Willow came in, I waved, and they joined us.
"Your turn for a round you tightwad. I'll have a Best, and a Vodka Coke for the lady"
"Fair point" I said "Can I say hi first?"
"Come here" we hugged, and suddenly the world was ever so slightly better.
"Hi Willow, good to see you" I said as we did the whole cheek kiss thing.
"You too. Looking happy today. That's good"
"Feel great today, thank you"
"Same again?" I asked Chrissy, and she nodded.
I left her to the hugging and went over to the bar to get the round in.
I'd repeat this trip another 3 times before the night was over, and Steve the same. Between us, we had racked up quite the collection of empty glasses by the end of the night. Felt like it too; I was half drunk. Partly from the booze, and partly from the

natural high I was still on. Chrissy was no better, and we made our way home in a most comical fashion.

We'd had a great day, and a great night. Steve didn't disappoint, and was extremely entertaining, teaching the ladies some new swear words. Willow and Chrissy were able to catch up on whatever women talk about, and I just enjoyed the show.

The comedy continued after we got home. As merry as I was, Chrissy was a bit further gone. She was quite funny. On our way up to bed, she turned on the stairs, waving a finger, saying "No funny business tonight Beckett", and proceeded to fall back, right into me, giggling like mad. I just about managed to hold on to the bannister to stop us both tumbling down the stairs. She just giggled, regained her balance, and carried on. I got to the bedroom after brushing my teeth, and she was sprawled out on the bed. Fast asleep. "No funny business indeed!" I said. There was no response.

I was able to stay awake for a while, just reflecting on how good this day had been. I considered headphones, but just cuddled up to the beautiful sleeping lump next to me. What a woman.

Welterusten.

Side notey.

You'll have to accept my apologies if the counsellor

visit wasn't 100% accurate, realistic, or whatever; I've never been. I was never strong enough to do so. I did like writing that bit, and it just flowed out without stopping. I felt good afterwards. Maybe not as good as Jack, but good enough. It was like a pseudo visit for myself. If you had the strength to go to a therapist or counsellor; kudos. I'm proud of you. You should be proud of yourself. You did more than me.

I wish I were as brave as you.

DAY 17

Tuesday, 2nd of April.

Ugh, my head hurts. You fucking penis. Serves you right. Yeah, you're right. Ok, let's go. One, two, three……open eyes. Ugh, it was bright; the sun was out. Normally I would have loved it, but right now, it could do one; my head was splitting. I turned, and saw that Chrissy was gone. Fuck. What time is it?? I looked at the clock; 09.34. Fuck. I had to get up and get to work. Come on Jack, get the fuck out!

I dragged myself out of bed, and went off to see where Chrissy was. She was probably in a worse state than me bless her. Singing from downstairs indicated otherwise. What the fuck? No. Surely not? I went down, and yes, there she was. Singing along to the radio in the kitchen.

"Oh hey, morning sleepy, how's the head?"

I winced "It's killing me" I said squinting.

"Here" she nodded towards a pint of water and two headache tablets. I guzzled down the water and took the tablets. "Ugh, I feel like shit" I said. "Thank you"

She laughed "You look like shit"
"Cheers"
"You want breakfast?"
I shook my head "No. No thanks. I'm going to have a shower"
"Ok" she laughed, and watched me walk back upstairs, ever so gingerly.
On my God. The shower was good. A Chinese doctor had told me once that hot shower on the back of the neck alleviates headaches. He was right. I stood for ten or so minutes with hot water blasting the back of my neck. Ugh, it felt good. I got out, dried off, and dressed. *No run today?* Fuck no.
I opened the curtains, and the room flooded with light. There was still pain, but nowhere near the levels of earlier. The sun was out, and it looked like a lovely day out there. I felt arms slipping around my waist and embracing me. "Feeling better?"
"Oh yeah, a lot. How are you?" I asked
"I'm fine, bit dehydrated, but no handover" she said proudly
"Fuck sake" I muttered, shaking my head.
"Poor baby, probably because you were so high on life yesterday"
"Hmmm." I said "Probably right. I don't usually feel this bad after a night out"
"Right" she said, slapping my backside "Stop feeling sorry for yourself. You've got work to do, chop chop."
"You're right." I said "I've got a shit tonne of stuff to do this week"

"Best get to it then. I've got to go into the city this morning, but will be back around one. You going to be ok?"
"Yeah, I'll be fine."
"Ok" she kissed me "See you later. Call if you need anything". She picked up her bag, and disappeared off out.
Silence fell over the house. Deathly silence. I took a deep breath, and went up to the office to get to work. Got to get occupied, get away from the silence. I put some music on to try ward off the silent mist all around me. It did the job, it retreated and left me a clear space to work in. Big sigh. Why though? I have nothing to be down about. *Come on Jack! Stop thinking and get to work.* Ok, ok. You're right. Deep breath. Ok. *So get on with it!* I am. Y*ou're sitting there staring into space, that's not good Jack. Not good at all.* I'm trying. *You call that trying? Jesus. Get a grip. Come on.* COME ON!!! Wow, ok, no need to shout. *I didn't dickwad, you did.* Shit. No. Not going to let this happen. Not today. Fuck off. Just fuck off!!!! *Mate, you gotta stop shouting.* I....oh. Shit. *Yo!* What? D*o me a favour?* What? *Go and take a pill. Like now.* Yeah, good idea. Good idea.
I went to the bedroom and got a popped a pill from the strip in my bedside drawer. I took it with a gulp of water. There. Done. *Good lad Jack, good lad. Now get back upstairs.* Ok. And, erm, thanks. *You're welcome. You know I'm not real and it's all you doing this right?* Sadly, I do.
I went back to the office, and got to work.

I had a text from Chrissy about an hour or so later, just checking up on me. I responded, telling her I was fine. Work was keeping me busy. Se reaffirmed that she'd be home around one ish.

Usual text from mum, asking if I was ok. I text back saying I was fine, and having a good day. *You fucking liar! Lol.* Yeah, whatever. I made a mental note to have a chat with mum to let her know I was having counselling. Sometime later in the week. Was almost done with one of the long factory tour videos, so got back to it.

Lunchtime came and went. I was still lost in work and didn't even notice until the doorbell rang.

I went down and answered it; the postman. Signature needed for this letter Jack. I signed, closed the door, and stared at it for a moment. *You ok jack? Hey, Jack! You good?* What? Oh, erm, yeah. I'm good. *What is it? And don't tell me it's a fucking letter dipshit.* Well, it is a letter, from Helen. *From Helen? What the fuck does she want?* I don't know. *You gonna open it maybe, and find out?* No. *What?* No. I put the letter in a kitchen cupboard; I didn't want to see it. I went back up to the office. *Hey, what the fuck you doing fucknut?* I'm not going to open it. Just leave it and let me get back to work. *What?* Leave it! *Ok, no need to shout.* I wasn....ah. Yeah I was. Fuck sake.

I sighed, and got back to work. The letter was soon out of my head. Work lasted until about three, then I'd just had enough. It was becoming a drag, and I

knew it was time to call it a day. House was still quiet. I thought Chrissy would be home by now. I checked my phone; she was still in the city, sorry.
So I was at a loose end. I grabbed my coat and went over to see Steve and Willow.
It wasn't raining, but the skies were grey. It was still cold out, but nowhere near freezing. The puddles were disappearing, and it was starting to look like a typical early spring. Some flowers were popping up here and there, and the expectancy of spring was in the air. I looked through the window, and saw the café was basically empty. One lady was sat nursing a coffee, no doubt just needing somewhere to be around people. Sitting at home, likely alone, was not good for the mind. Bless her. I sympathised. She was like me. I was like her. We needed company for our sanity.

Tinkle.
"Afternoon sunshine" Wait. No swearing?
"Afternoon" I said, uncertain. "How's tricks?"
"All good mate, how's you?
"Sure? You usually come here when you're not"
Willow came walking in from the kitchen "Stephen, leave the man alone. Hi Jack, good to see you"
"Hey Willow, how are you doing?"
"I'm good thanks. Don't mind this fool, he's just worried about you"
"Hey, I am here you know" Steve said
"Latte?" Willow asked.

"Yes please, if that's ok"
"Sure, sit yourself down."
"You want anything to eat before it gets ditched?" Steve asked
"You ditch your food? You know there are starving people out there right?" I said
"Mate, I have 3 pastries left, hardly going to end world hunger. You want some or not?"
"Yes please"
"All of them?"
"Mate, I'm starving, so yes please"
"Ok, go sit"
I went to my table, and sat down. My phone buzzed; message from Chrissy. She was on her way home. I text back and told her I was here, and would save her a pastry.
"Here, enjoy" Willow said, smiling as she brought my coffee over.
"Thank you" I picked up the cup, enjoying the heat in my hands.
"Hey man, here, get stuck in" Steve said, putting a plate in front of me.
"Thanks bud"
He sat.
"You got a moment?"
I looked around "Erm yeah…"
"Just wanna pick your brain about something."
"Ok, shoot" I said, sipping my coffee. It was superb.
"So, I had a chat with Lenoir yesterday, and she had an interesting proposition."
"Lenoir now is it?" I smiled "What proposition?"

"We talked about assets, how to maximise my profit, and all that bollocks. So basically, we talked about moving the caff."

"From here to where?" I asked

"Her aunt's place" he said hesitantly

"Makes sense" I said "You sure you'd get the same level of custom there?"

"To be honest mate, I could be located anywhere and they would still come."

"True" He was right, it wouldn't matter where the caff was; the ladies would still come.

"So we talked about custom too, and we had an idea"

"Yes....."

"We can set up the house as a café, and run the two at the same time for a transitional period. I think that's what she said."

"Makes perfect sense mate" I said, nodding my agreement

"You think?"

"Yeah, we have time to decorate the house, and then run both for a bit."

"I'd have to get a new coffee machine, but other than that, I don't think there's a lot else."

"It's bigger for sure" I said "You can use upstairs for office and storage space, and possibly the back garden as a terrace?" The Willow Tree, whilst lovely, was a single story building, without garden space. "You going to sell this place?"

"Well, rent it out" he said "Already have a taker"

"Wow, that's quick" I said

"The plan is complicated mate, but should work. Simply put, I'm renting Lenoir's place, and she's renting mine." He looked at me "Make sense"
"Kind of." I said. "What she going to use this place for?" I asked
"I'll let her tell you that mate, not sure if she wanted me to mention it to you" he said, worried.
"Ah, like that is it? Ok mate, I'll ask her when she gets here in a bit"
"Exciting though right?" he said
"Yes mate, big change. It's a better location for you for sure"
"It is, I'm pretty excited"
"Good for you mate, I'm really happy for you"

Tinkle

"Oh, I'll leave you to it" he whispered "Afternoon Lenoir, you good?"
"Better than good Stephen" she winked, waved at me quickly, then went to say hi to Willow.
A moment later, we were hugging. "Hi, busy day?" I asked
"Wow, yeah, super busy. I'm pooped" she said with a smile "How's work going? You feeling better?"
"Yeah, I'm good ta. Work, well I had to stop as I just ran out of steam, hence I'm here"
"Good. Oh, thanks Willow, you're a life saver" she said as Willow brought over a large Latte for her.
"Welcome" she smiled and trotted off.
"Here" I said, "I saved you some pastries"
"Oh, great, I'm starving" she said and ate greedily

"So" I said "Had an interesting chat with Steve just now"

"Ah. Yeah." she said, with a tinge of guilt. "I didn't want to say anything until I had researched it properly. Hence I'm late today" she sipped her coffee "I went to see my solicitor to talk it through, and it's all pretty straightforward apparently. Not difficult to set up"

"Well, Steve will be more than happy to hear that" I said

"He seemed excited about it, but I told him to keep it to himself" she said, loudly, turning to Steve.

"Soz" he said, shrugging.

"Men, can't be trusted with anything!"

"You got that right" Willow agreed.

"So what did he tell you?" she asked, turning back to me

"Just about moving the caff, and running two for a transition or something?"

"Yeah, we talked about that, but not sure it makes sense. Why run two? Just close for a few days and have a grand re-opening"

"That makes far more sense" I agreed.

"He tell you about the rental agreement?"

"Nope" I lied

"Liar"

"Me?"

"Yes, I can tell." she winked "Anyway. My idea was to kind of swap premises so he had a bigger place for the café and the garden."

"And you would have?" I asked, leading….

"An office space" she said smiling
"An office space? You moving your operation there?"
"No. Not me."
"Oh?"
"You are" she said.
"What?" I asked confused
"Your office will be there" she said proudly
"Mine?" I said, still confused "But I have an office?"
"Think about it Jack; what happens when you're home alone? In the quiet, empty house?"
"I crash" I said, ashamed
"Hey, no, not meant to shame you. I was thinking you would benefit from being out of the house"
"OK...."
"Well, I can work from anywhere, and the home office is perfect for me. You need somewhere away from there Jack. Think about it. I think it would be good for you"
She was right. I liked the idea of it. Being out of the house was good. True, I'd still be alone off-site, but I wouldn't be in the house. The house isn't the issue, the empty house it the issue.
"I like it" I said eventually
"Yeay!" she said clapping her hands together. "It'll be good. Well put an office, kitchen bathroom and gym room in"
"A gym room?" I asked, eyebrows raised
"Yep, you can take breaks to work out, or run, have a shower, and go back to work."
"I really like the idea of that" I said "A lot"

I leaned across the table and kissed her "Thank you"
"You're welcome" she said "It's going to be great"
My mood level had gone from negative to sky high. One thing was worrying me though.
"Why can't we share the office space?"
"No." clinical.
"What? Why not?"
"My love, we would end up killing each other if we worked together. It's not healthy."
"Good point. You'd end up doing my head in" I said
Shoulder punch.
"Definitely deserved that." she said.

We made our way home, and Chrissy said we should celebrate with a takeaway and a few beers.
That sounds like a great idea.
We showered and changed, and drove over to Ramsey to get an Indian. There is only one, so we didn't have much choice; we went in, and ordered.
"You sure you're happy with my ideas?" she asked as we walked back to the car.
"Of course I am, and I'm very grateful. I'll just have to figure out how to finance it. Shouldn't be a problem"
"It isn't a problem; I'll make it happen" she said
"What? No, I'll help out, it's not an issue"
"Hey. Let me. I have money from selling my flat, I can afford it. Besides, I get my own office out of it too"
I wasn't in a position to argue, and she knew it. My

finances weren't great at the moment. There was no way I could finance this.

"Thank you" I said

"Ach, we're a team, we help each other out right?"

"Right"

"Cool, now get us home before these curries go cold"

"Yes ma'am" I said, and drove us home.

We got home, and had a wonderful evening; the curries were superb, and the beers went down well. We watched a movie, and just enjoyed each other's company.

Once the movie was over, Chrissy got up and took all the take away containers to the kitchen.

I was sat finishing my beer, when she came back in.

"Hey" kiss. "What's this?" she had the letter in her hand. Fuck. I'd completely forgotten.

"It's from Helen. I don't want to open it" Shit. Shit. Shit.

"What? Why not? Could be important" she asked confused.

"Because it's going to be bad, and I don't want bad right now" I explained.

She looked puzzled, so I said "If you want to open it, go ahead. I'm not going to"

"You sure?" she asked

"Yes, knock yourself out"

"Ok" she said and disappeared back out to the kitchen.

Holy fuck. I'd forgotten about the letter. *Dickhead!*

Why did you give it to her to read? Why not? *You have no idea what it is you penis.* Ach, it's probably just something about the kids right? Right? *Sure....*

It was eerily quiet. Did she read it? Maybe it was nothing.

You gonna ask? What, now? *No, next week you knobber.* Sigh….

I got up and went out to ask. Chrissy was sat at the table, her head down, letter on the table in front of her.

"You read it?" I asked.

"Yes" she said quietly. Wait, were those tears? Oh shit. *Told you…*

"Hey, what is it?" I asked, my concern evident.

"Please don't do it" she said, tears rolling down her face.

What the fuck?

The End

OUTRO.

So? What did you think? Bit longer that the first instalment, and more focussed on the characters than on details of divorce. This book was a lot of fun to write. I hope you enjoyed reading it as much as I did writing it. It also brought back some buried feelings, but they're back underground.

The past is the past. Done, Gone. Can't change it. Accept & move on.

The character of Jack is broken, but finally getting help. Good for him. And he has a supportive partner to help him on his journey. I really hope if you're in the same situation that you have someone to support you. If you don't, you have my deepest sympathies. Some people think they're strong enough alone. No. Not true. If you dig deep, and some will have to excavate quite far down, past all that pride, you'll find it's true. You need someone. Doesn't have to be a lover; could be a friend, or someone on the end of a phone. It's good to share. It feels good to share. Even after all these years, I love talking to other guys that have come through a bad divorce; we always have a fantastic chat, and we always feel better after.

But, I should stop there. Don't want to drone on too much.

I left you hanging on the edge of a cliff at the end of Day 17. What's in the letter?
Well, you'll have to wait for part III....

In the meantime,

Be good, and look after yourself.

Mike.

08 Mar 2024.